ODIN'S QUEEN

SUSAN PRICE

ALSO BY SUSAN PRICE:

Odin's Voice

ODIN'S QUEEN

SUSAN PRICE

SIMON & SCHUSTER

First published in Great Britain in 2006 by Simon & Schuster UK Ltd
A CBS Company

Text copyright © 2006 Susan Price
Cover illustration by Larry Rostant © Simon & Schuster 2006
Cover title lettering by www.blacksheep-uk.com

This paperback edition published in 2007.

www.susanprice.org.uk

1 3 5 7 9 10 8 6 4 2

Simon & Schuster UK Ltd
Africa House
64-78 Kingsway
London WC2B 6AH

www.simonsays.co.uk

A CIP catalogue record for this book is available from the British Library

ISBN-10: 1416904441
ISBN-13: 9781416904441

This book is a work of fiction. Names, characters, places and incidents
are either a product of the author's imagination or are used fictitiously.
Any resemblance to actual people living or dead, events or locales
is entirely coincidental.

Typeset by Palimpsest Book Production Limited,
Grangemouth, Stirlingshire
Printed and bound in Great Britain by
Cox & Wyman, Reading, Berks

The Journey

'Tell me again,' said Affie. 'Who is the blue bead . . .?'

'My great-grandmother,' Odinstoy said.

'That's your mother's mother's mother, right? And her name . . .?'

'Don't know,' said Odinstoy, bored.

'Not at *all*?'

'I know she tied that bead on the string for me.'

'What if she had other children?' Affie said. 'And what if she made ancestor strings for them? She wouldn't have the same things to tie on, would she?' Bonders had to make use of what they could get. 'You could have met your—' She wasn't sure what relation your great-grandmother's children would be to yourself. 'One of your family. And you wouldn't know.'

Odinstoy shrugged.

'I know all my ancestors' names,' Affie said. 'Well, if I can't remember them, they're all in the tree.' Her silver ancestor tree, with its dangling photographs, and the small computer in its base, was tucked into one of the drawers under her bed. 'And what they did and who they married

1

and *everything*. Who is the locket?' Affie was fingering Odinstoy's ancestor string, counting off the things tied on it.

'My grandmother.'

'And her name?'

'Don't know. But that's her picture inside.'

Affie prised open the cheap, scratched locket and looked at the hologram inside. 'She was pretty. And the Freya medal, that's for your mother, right?'

'Right.'

'And this bit of stone—'

'It's an arrow.'

'Whatever,' Affie said peaceably, while thinking: Who would make an arrow out of stone? It would be too heavy. Besides, it had no – well, stick, or stalk, or whatever you called that part of an arrow. But Odinstoy, for all her talents, was really only a bonder. Whatever she'd been told, she'd believe, knowing no better. 'But that's you, right? You tied it on for Apollo?'

'That's right.'

Apollo, the little brat – she had to remember to call him 'Odinsgift' now. He was the reason for them being on their way to Mars. The reason for everything, really. Odinstoy had only befriended Affie because of her precious Apollo – no, *Odinsgift*. She had only helped Affie escape because Affie had been able to steal the boy away from his adoptive parents and bring him with her.

Sometimes, when what she was doing came to her fully, Affie went cold right through to the centre of her bones. She was a bonder, and a bonder running away was bad enough. She was stealing herself from her owners. But she had kidnapped their child too. She didn't want to think about what the punishment would be if she was caught, but the possibilities paraded through her mind anyway: re-education; years of imprisonment; maybe even hanging. She felt her heart squeeze small within her.

Then she would think of what her life would be if she *hadn't* run away. Day after day of miserable drudgery, of not ever being allowed to be herself. Displays of pleasure, or anger, or unhappiness – any emotion, really – were 'not suitable' in a bonder. And she would grow old, and life would have passed her by, and she would never have had any life except the cramped one of a bonder.

Sometimes that made her feel better because, no matter what happened, she'd had no choice but to take the only chance open to her. Sometimes she went on feeling scared and sick for hours. Now, because she was with Odinstoy, and because the ship's lights were on brightly, for day, she shook off the spasm of fear, and went on counting off the ancestor string.

'Great-Granny, Granny, Mummy, Odinstoy. I know all your ancestors now, as well as my own.' Of course, there were far fewer of Odinstoy's. 'I think I might throw mine away.'

At least *that* made Odinstoy turn her intense, dark, Japanese eyes Affie's way. 'Throw away your ancestors?'

'Why not? What use will they be to me on Mars?' Everything would be new and better and free on Mars.

3

On Mars they would be rich. And free. On Mars they would be able to stamp and rage, or laugh or cry and be their own true, free selves. So why not throw away her ancestors, together with all the rest of her old life, and start afresh?

It wasn't as if her ancestors had ever been of any use to her. Her father had killed himself, just because he'd run into difficulties with a few debts. Had he given a thought to her? No, and she'd been sold, along with the rest of his estate. It hadn't bothered him, because he'd been safely dead. Laughing and enjoying himself in the afterlife, or just unknowing, in oblivion, depending on what you believed. Either way, it made no difference to her. She hadn't been laughing and enjoying herself, or been in oblivion. She'd been thrown, unprepared, from a life of spoilt comfort into the life of a bonder, and she'd been miserable.

And her mother, Freewoman bloody Lloyd – she'd taken herself off to America and a new husband and hadn't even bothered to send her good wishes when Affie had desperately texted her for help.

There were grandparents on her mother's side, but they were as useless as her mother – she hadn't seen or heard from them since she'd been four, five, something like that.

The rest of her ancestors, the whole crowd, the whole roll-call of them, were all dead and all useless. They were supposed to watch over her from the afterlife and help her out – but either that wasn't true, or they were all like her mother and father, and the most useless, idle, ineffectual

4

bunch of ancestors anyone had ever been cursed with. Odinstoy's ancestors may all have been bonders, but they seemed a much more capable bunch. Favourites of the great God, Odin, too. Odin had got her and Toy away from Earth, hadn't he?

Her own ancestors were just silver-framed photos and names and facts logged in a computer's memory: something to brag about, nothing more.

It was Odinstoy who'd saved her from bondery; Odinstoy who was taking her to Mars. 'Why don't I share your ancestors? You said we'd go to Mars as sisters.'

Odinstoy laughed. 'And we're going as husband and wife!' It had seemed to make sense. The authorities would be looking for two women and a kidnapped child, so if they travelled as man and wife, with their son, that should make them more difficult to spot. Odinstoy had often dressed as a man before, when she'd spoken for Odin in the temple; and she made a convincing, if short and slight, young man.

Affie had to be the wife, because she could never have passed for a man. Her parents had paid for her to be genetically designed before birth and she was, she knew, a very beautiful young woman. She was slim, but still curvy, with long legs, and her hormones and metabolism had been delicately balanced, so that she'd have to eat like three horses before she would put on any weight. Her skin had always been clear, and was a lovely, warm caramel shade. Her face was oval, with big dark-brown eyes, a full-lipped mouth, and a little pointed chin. Her long, slightly wavy, glossy hair was a couple of shades darker than her skin, and was full of shifting cloud-shapes and colours that changed according to her mood – the genetic engineers had added jellyfish genes to her mix to get the effect. When she was happy or angry, the cloud-shapes were warm and quick, ranging from orange through pinks and reds to bright scarlet. When she was unhappy, they slowed and cooled, sinking through greens, violets and blues to indigo. Even in the disguise she'd worn for their escape – dark, dowdy clothes, and a wig to cover her sparkling hair – she was still beautiful.

'Don't throw your ancestors away,' Odinstoy said. 'They're silver. Worth money. And more than money.'

'How?'

'People will think a lot more of you because of that fancy ancestor tree than they'll think of me and my bits on a string. That's for bonders. Only the free have fancy ancestor trees.'

'And jumped-up ex-bonders,' Affie said, quite oblivious to the fact that she was herself an ex-bonder. In her own mind she had never *really* been a bonder, but only a princess, cast down temporarily from her true place. 'Will you get yourself a fancy ancestor tree when we're on Mars, when we're rich?' Affie was quite sure they were going to be rich on Mars. And famous. And admired. They'd be free; they could do anything if they wanted it enough. 'You could invent a few more ancestors, to fill it out. You could have some of mine.'

Odinstoy gave her a long straight look. 'I'm not free,

never will be. I'm owned by Odin. On Earth, on Mars, I'm Odin's Toy.'

It took three Earth months to make the passage to Mars. Ninety Earth days. That didn't sound so long. Affie thought it would soon pass. They had Mars and freedom to look forward to.

The first couple of weeks had gone quickly enough. They had been learning the lay-out and routine of the ship, and had still been gleeful over their escape from Earth, and full of anticipation about Mars. There had been the amusement of finding themselves much lighter than they were on Earth – the ship had artificial gravity, but it was weak. They could bound along corridors and lounges, leaping up to touch the ceiling or pirouetting in mid-air.

Affie was disappointed with the ship. She'd thought a great ship, sailing to Mars, would be something special. Of course, she'd reminded herself that she wouldn't be in Executive, or VIP. She wasn't rich any more but she wasn't a bonder either! She was *supposed* to be a free God-speaker's wife – surely the Martian Temple of Odin could have paid for something half decent?

They had their little cabin – a double, though it was a double cubby-hole. There were bunk-beds, with a cot for Gift; and a tiny table and chair. That was it. There wasn't even anywhere to wash. They had to share communal lavatories and sonic showers, which Affie thought was disgusting. She couldn't help thinking that, when she used the showers, she was standing in all the skin and hair that had been shaken off the hundreds of people who'd used them before her.

There was a dining room where everyone ate together at big tables; and they had to go to a serving hatch to collect their food. At least they didn't have to cook it – someone in the kitchens reheated it. The stuff wasn't much good.

'That's why they give us so much laughing-juice with it,' said an elderly, jovial man, who was returning with his wife from a trip to Earth. Like all Martians, they were tall, and they didn't seem to mind looking old. They'd taken their trip, he said, 'to see the Mother of us all'.

There were big lounges with easy chairs, computers, screens, and snack-drink machines. And there was a gym, which all passengers were urged to use regularly, because the ship's weak gravity reduced stress on their bones and weakened them. Therefore, they should stress their bones as much possible, to maintain them.

'Three months won't make much difference,' their friend Thorsgift said. 'But the company like to protect themselves. Wait till you get to Mars!'

'Oh, I felt so heavy on Earth!' said the elderly man's wife. 'I could hardly move! It was fun to see Earth, but I can't wait to be home, to be honest.'

By the end of two weeks Affie knew every inch of the ship. She knew every one of her fellow passengers, all but a few of them lanky Martians. She'd watched films and programmes, played games – games and films which seemed more and more dreary and stupid when she found herself watching the same plots or playing the same games yet again. The games induced a strange state of mind: intense interest in the outcome and, at the same time, intense boredom. Even while compelled to play on, the repetition scraped on the soul. And there were still ten weeks to go.

But she was on her way to Mars and freedom!

Eight weeks into the journey and they were still wearing the same clothes they'd boarded in, shabby from being constantly cleaned in the sonic showers. Every time they walked round the ship, they saw the same drink and snack machines, the same safety warnings, heard the same information messages warbling from the speakers – *'Stress isn't always bad! Your bones need stress to maintain their strength! So take our advice and stress your bones every day!'* – saw the same stain on the same wall (which you knew you were going to have to notice before you came near it), the same bit of threadbare carpet in the same doorway, the same unlit light in a row of lights . . . Affie had often been bored before, as a rich girl *and* as a bonder, but this was a new frontier of boredom. When she'd been rich, she could always go shopping or have her nails or hair done. When she'd been a bonder, she could concentrate on the hour of relief when the drudgery would end and she could go to bed for a few hours. But this boredom went on and on and on. And on and on. There was no way out until they reached Mars. In another two weeks. Fourteen days. Three hundred and thirty-six draggy hours. She longed for Mars.

Hours – days – weeks – were passed merely in talking. It was odd that the only person on the ship they already knew – Thorsgift – was almost the last person to speak to them. Affie supposed that you couldn't blame him. He'd been sent to Earth to find a God-speaker, had chosen Odinstoy, and had then found himself embroiled in a plot to kidnap a child from his legal parents and steal a bonder – Affie herself – from her owners, who happened to be the same bereaved parents.

As Odinstoy had forcefully said, she, Odinstoy, was the child's real mother, had carried him inside her, had birthed him, had done all the dirty work of caring for him in his first years of life. But because she had been, at the time, a bonder, her owners had legally been able to take him from her and call him their son. She was only, Odinstoy said, reclaiming what was rightfully hers, and she wouldn't go to Mars without him. And Affie had to come, because Affie was the current bonder who looked after Odinsgift.

Thorsgift hadn't been able to say no, because he'd fallen under the fascination that Odinstoy could cast. She'd cast it around Affie. It must be something to do with being a God-speaker, Affie thought, because it wasn't about looks. Affie was far more beautiful than Odinstoy, and *she* couldn't lead people along as Odinstoy could.

Thorsgift had helped them, but he hadn't been happy about it. He'd seen them when they'd boarded the Space-El – when they'd been allowed to board, after Security had questioned them and let them go – but he'd pretended not to know them.

As they'd drawn further away from Earth, he'd relaxed, and had started chatting, as if striking up a shipboard friendship. 'Have you worked out the time difference yet?'

They looked at him curiously.

'I'm fourteen,' he said, and grinned – a tall, bearded man.

An old man said, 'And I'm thirty-two.'

Affie was half smiling, not sure why they were saying these ridiculous things.

'A Martian year is nearly twice as long as an Earth year,' Thorsgift said.

'Don't worry, though,' the old man's wife said. 'The sol's about the same as a day.'

'"Sol" is the Mars word for "day",' Thorsgift said.

Odinstoy said nothing, but Affie snapped, 'We *know*!'

'And what's *your* name?' the old lady said to Odinstoy's son.

He stopped running up and down the lounge for a moment, stared at her, and said, 'Odinsgift.'

Apollo had learned very quickly to answer to 'Odinsgift' or 'Gift'. It was Affie who had slipped up a few times and called him 'Pollo'.

'New blood's always welcome on Mars,' said the woman, as she stared at Odinstoy, looked away, then stared again. She looked at Affie and smiled. 'Settle in, and then come and see us.'

Affie was amused. She was used to people admiring her and smiling – they'd done it since she was a child. Now they were well on their way to Mars, she left off the

11

dowdy dark wig. Her own hair, which had been regularly shaved as a bonder, was growing back in attractive curls and waves, and colours shimmered through it in cloud-patterns. Of course people wanted to know her better.

But Odinstoy fascinated people even more. Affie had seen it before, and could see it now, in the way their fellow passengers stared and peeped at her; in the way people's attention would be drawn to her whenever she entered a public room. Most of it, of course, was because they weren't sure whether she was a man or a woman – because she was nothing to look at, as either sex. Her face wasn't pretty, though Affie supposed it could be called 'striking'. It was so broad across the cheekbones that it seemed round; with very dark brows and lashes, a pale skin, and almond-shaped eyes. You'd take them for dark, those eyes; but then, in a different light, you'd realise that they were greenish, or hazel; and finally, leaning close, you would see, with surprise, that they were a dark grey, or slate-blue.

Odinstoy's figure was quite stocky and blocky – though she was small and thin she was also short-limbed, flat-chested and almost waistless. That was why she made a quite convincing man, at first. But when they lived at close quarters with her for a long time, people began to notice the smallness of her hands and feet, and her lack of an Adam's apple, and they wondered. Of course, no one would ask or say anything, but Affie saw them glancing at each other. Odinstoy must have been aware of their curiosity too, because she removed it by calling Gift to her, saying, 'Come to Mummy.' And Affie overheard her saying casually to one of the Martian women, 'I've lived as a man for ten years now.' A lie, but Odinstoy lied whenever it suited her.

Within a couple of hours of being on the ship, everyone knew that Odinstoy was a woman who lived as a man, and Affie found it very annoying to see how interested the other men suddenly were. It made Affie jealous. (*She* wanted to be the most special person in Odinstoy's life, not any man – which was another reason to dislike the brat Apollo, or Odinsgift, or whatever she was supposed to call him.)

Men always seemed to find Odinstoy beguiling, for some reason. Back on Earth, Bob Sing and Markus had both helped them escape because they were fascinated by Odinstoy. And Thorsgift had chosen Odinstoy for Mars's new God-speaker, and had helped them leave Earth, because he was fascinated by Odinstoy – and still was. He mooned about her, quickly joining her whenever she appeared, fetching her coffee, trying to sit next to her, trying to win her attention away from whoever or whatever else had gained it. He became more and more obviously smitten the further they went from Earth, and his fear of the Earth authorities weakened. He and Affie would smile at each other from either side of Odinstoy with hatred in their eyes.

'I'm Church of Mars myself,' said a man. 'Got to be, for my job, y'know. But we'll be sure to come and hear you preach.'

'Your little boy is lovely,' said a woman, smiling at both Affie and Odinstoy. 'So pretty and lively.' Her smile brightened; her eyes flickered hopefully from one to the other. She longed to ask, but didn't quite dare, which one was the mother – Affie, the wife, or Odinstoy, the husband? Or was Gift the bio-engineered child of them both?

'We're very proud of him,' Affie said, thinking it the sort of thing she should say. Gift was playing on the floor nearby, with some model animals – dogs, pigs, sheep and cows. She could see why the woman would wonder. Gift was a solidly-built, stocky child, which perhaps gave him something of a likeness to Toy, but apart from that, he was not like either of them. His hair was thick and so fair it was almost white; and his large eyes were blue. His face was wide, ruddy and handsome.

'How old is he?' the woman asked.

'Er . . .' Affie looked at Toy.

'Four,' Toy said.

'Goodness! He's big for his age!' The woman glanced at her companion, and unsaid words hung in the air.

Affie could have supplied them: big for his age, and yet so backward in his speech. But not stupid, much as Affie would have liked to think so. He understood what was said to him quite readily, though he often wouldn't do as he was told, but he expressed himself as clumsily as a child half his age.

As a change from films and games and talk, they some-times went to the Observation Lounge and looked out at the eternity of space and stars. It was the only place on the ship where you could clearly see that you were on a *space*ship. Affie had thought she would spend a lot of time there, being spiritual and marvelling – but was soon appalled by the immensity, the coldness, the terrifying bleak beauty. A very few minutes of it sent her scurrying back to the cosiness of the lounge, with its tables, snack machines, chairs and cups of coffee. Seeing that most other passengers did the same made her feel better, and she would sit at a computer, designing clothes for herself, and forgetting about the vast, dark emptiness on the other side of the ship's thin hull. When they got to Mars, she thought, she might become a clothes designer, the most famous on the planet.

Odinstoy sat alone in Observation, in a padded seat, leaning forward, elbows on knees, staring at the stars.

Thorsgift had explained to her that the light reaching her eyes from these stars had been shining through emptiness for longer than her world had existed. The world it had left was already dead.

It was the mind of Odin spread out before her. Odin, who saw that the unchangeable future held nothing but death; yet still fought on, because it was better to die fighting than humbled.

It hurt to look at the darkness and the stars, because it made it so clear how unimportant and irrelevant she was – it made everyone feel that, which was why the Observation Lounge was empty apart from her. But the crushing feeling of insignificance turned, for Odinstoy, into a strange exhilaration and power. If nothing mattered, if nothing was important, then why be afraid? Of anything?

Still, she wondered why she was there. Why she'd wasted three months of her life to leave Earth and travel to Mars. She could have stolen Gift and gone to another town on Earth, or another country. There were places on Earth where she could stare at the stars and feel unafraid.

She asked Odin: Why did You want me to come to Mars?

The answer welled up in her mind, like a head rising from the depths of the pool at the World Tree's roots. *Because I wished you to come.*

But why? Odinstoy persisted. *Why* did You want me to come?

In time, you will know, came the answer. *Or, if you never know, it won't matter. For now, speak for Me. That's all I ask.*

Outside, endlessly, the stars glittered. Her eyes on them, Odinstoy nodded. 'I am Your Toy.'

The door to Observation, which often stuck, rattled as it was hauled open. 'In here again,' Affie said, looking in. 'You're wanted.'

'Who wants me?'

'The Captain. And I wish you wouldn't go off and leave your brat with me.'

Odinstoy stood. 'Why does the Captain want me?'

Seeing her face, Affie said, 'Oh, don't worry. It's something about Radio Mars.'

Gift was running up and down the short corridor

outside Observation. He had altogether too much energy, in Affie's view. Seeing his mother, he ran at her, almost knocking her down.

'*Don't* run at Toy like that!' Affie scolded. 'You're getting a big boy.'

'Leave him,' Toy said, and took his hand.

What could you do?

Affie followed.

The 'control room' of the ship was a cupboard, with a couple of chairs squeezed in. The Captain was already seated in one chair – his title was 'Captain', but he often joked that he was no more than a glorified steward. Computers steered and controlled the ship. 'Ah, Odinstoy! Come in, come in. Take a seat.'

Toy took the empty seat, heaving Gift onto her lap. Affie leaned against the wall beside her, pulling the door shut after them. There was just enough room for them all.

'I've got Radio Mars on the line,' the Captain said. 'They'd like to talk to you, if that's all right.'

'Why?' Toy said.

He looked surprised. 'You're going to be a God-speaker there, aren't you? For – Hermes, is it?'

'Odin,' Affie snapped. You'd think the man would know. They'd been on the ship for nearly three months.

'Yeah, yeah, Odin. Is it OK if they speak with you? They're just – well, they're like, somebody new coming to Mars – a God-speaker. It's a big deal down there. They know all their listeners will be interested. So – is it OK?'

Toy said nothing. Affie bent forward to see her face. 'Yes! Go on. You'll be, like, famous.'

Toy stared blankly ahead of her, while Gift slipped from her lap and started to examine the console. Affie, seeing the Captain become nervous, grasped Gift by the neck of his shirt, opened the door again, and hauled him out. It wasn't easy: he was a heavy, strong child. But she succeeded in bundling him out and shutting the door on him. He shrieked and kicked the door but then, evidently, something or someone distracted him, because he was quiet.

In her head Odinstoy was thinking: I don't want to do this. Do I have to do it?

Odin's answer was: *Do it.*

'All right,' Odinstoy said.

'Excellent!' said the Captain. 'Mikes open.' He flicked a switch. 'Hello there, Merc. I've got Odinstoy here. He says he'll do it.'

A voice, unexpectedly loud, burst from speakers, making both Odinstoy and Affie jump. '*Oh, super! Good sol, Odinstoy!*'

Odinstoy crossed one ankle over the other knee, stared at the console, and said nothing.

'*Odinstoy?*' the speakers boomed.

Affie leaned forward. 'Good sol, Mars! We're so happy to be almost there!'

'*Hello?*' boomed the speakers, sounding puzzled. '*Is that Odinstoy?*'

Odinstoy smiled, but didn't answer.

The Captain started to speak, but Affie cut through him. 'No, I'm Affie – that's Affroditey – er – Atkinson. Hello! Good sol! Odinstoy's here, she's just not speaking. Odinstoy – say something!'

Odinstoy leaned back and grinned.

The speakers said, 'She? *We were told—* Who is that speaking, please?'

The Captain and Affie answered almost together.

'Odinstoy's companion.'

'Oh, I'm Affie, Odinstoy's – ah – wife.'

The speakers said, '*Who? Wife?*' There was a moment of confused silence, then: '*I've got "Freya" as the name of Odinstoy's wife?*'

'That's right – I am Freya Atkinson, but my middle name's Affroditey, and I was always called Affie, you see.'

Another silence. '*Is Odinstoy there? Can I speak to – er . . .?*'

'I am Odin's Toy. I speak for Odin to all. I speak for all to Odin.'

'*Oh. Er. Good,*' said the speakers.

'Because I speak for all, I live as a man, though I'm a woman. I am the mother of a son, and the husband of a girl.'

'*Oh,*' said the speakers. '*Jolly good! Can I ask you a few questions for our listeners?*'

'Ask,' Odinstoy said. 'Maybe Odin will answer.'

'*Oh. Super! I'll fire away then, shall I?*'

Zeuslove

It was a curious voice, hard to place. *'Odin called me to Mars,'* it said, *'so I came.'*

The speaker came from Earth and spoke English, that much was clear; but Zeuslove wasn't familiar enough with the nuances of Earth accents to be able to tell anything more. The language meant nothing. English was the main language of Earth and Mars.

The voice was both soft and hoarse, suddenly scratching throatily at the hearing in a rather seductive way . . . Which was disturbing, because it could have been the voice of a boy or a woman.

'Did Odin give you a mission?' the interviewer asked eagerly.

'He said I was to come.' The voice sounded irritated at having to repeat this: indeed, the speaker seemed reluctant to answer at all. *'I'm His Toy. Whatever He asks, I do.'*

Zeuslove Thatcher slapped his hand on his desk, and said, 'Oh, the loving Gods!' Then he silenced himself, listening.

'*You were a bonder on Earth, is that true?*' asked the interviewer.

'*She was freed!*' said another voice, unmistakeably a girl's voice.

'*Yes, but you* were *a bonder?*'

'*I was born a bonder,*' the boyish, husky voice agreed. '*Odin taught me to speak for Him while I was bonded. Then He freed me. To come to Mars.*'

So intense was Zeuslove's distaste that he wriggled in his chair and grimaced. 'A bonder. A bonder!'

'*I understand you have your wife with you, Odinstoy,*' said the interviewer.

'*Hi!*' said the girl's voice.

'*Hi! Won't you introduce yourself?*'

'*Hi, everyone. I'm Freya Atkinson, Odinstoy's wife – but call me "Affie", it's my middle name.*'

'*Right you are, Affie. How long have you and Odinstoy been married?*'

'*We married when I was given to Odin,*' Odinstoy said.

'*And you have a young son, am I right?*'

'*He is my son,*' Odinstoy said. '*I am his mother and father.*' Zeuslove, listening, gave a small start of surprise. '*I am my wife's husband and sister. I—*'

'Tcha!' Zeuslove couldn't keep quiet. 'Command! Close!'

The computer stopped the recording. Zeuslove fidgeted at his desk, swung to and fro in his chair, picked up pens, scissors, photographs, and put them down again

A God-speaker for Odin, coming from Earth. A *bonder*, speaking for Odin, from Earth. It wasn't good.

And a woman married to a woman! A woman bonder, pretending to be a man, pretending to be married to a woman, pretending to speak for Odin! It was so outrageous, so ludicrous, it was almost funny – but the fact that this freakish pervert was actually landing on Mars in a few sols' time made it obscene, not funny.

What were her pretences and charades likely to teach the young, the impressionable?

As if Mars didn't have enough immoral low-lifes of its own, without importing more from Earth. And Odin!

The Gods knew, worshipping Odin was, in itself, bad enough. But a woman and a bonder claiming to speak for Odin! In effect, she was claiming – *a woman and a bonder* – to know the Mind of Zeus.

Zeuslove shook his head. He just didn't have words for the folly of it. The pitiful and brazen folly. The blasphemy. The obscene blasphemy and intolerable pretension.

His church was the Church of Mars, the true faith of Earth transplanted to the junior planet. He had served it since boyhood with study, prayers, and sacrifices, and he loved it because of its great age, stretching back through so many centuries. Nothing false could have survived so long, as so many faddy, fashionable little cults had proved, springing up and then dying within a hundred years or so. But the Great, the Eternal Gods – Zeus and Hera, Aphrodite and Ares, Artemis and Apollo, Hermes, Dionysus, Demeter, Persephone, Hades – these went on for ever.

All his life he'd worked with the people of the Church,

comforting, bringing those in need together with those who needed to give help. He had made friendships with the priests and priestesses of Demeter, Hermes, Apollo, Artemis and others, so strengthening and building the community. He had earned respect, and his fellow priests had honoured him by asking him to step into the place of Zeus's Archpriest on Mars. Youngsters wishing to serve Zeus wished to do so under his guidance. He had been asked to be a councillor of his canton, and was now a member of the Council of Mars. His face and words were often broadcast.

It was a little, frail colony that lived on Mars, even after three hundred years. It was his colony, his family. Every child born on Mars was precious, and was his child, his responsibility. They all – everyone who lived on Mars – had a responsibility to build a community that would nourish itself, and grow strong and thrive. There was no time or space for wrongness. And as a leader of the community, he, Zeuslove, had a greater responsibility than most to speak out. To lead.

Mars needed clear guidance, clear rules, firm boundaries. The godless forever tried to confuse matters but, in truth, it was not difficult to distinguish right from wrong. The difference should be set out clearly, for everyone to understand, and no excuses should be accepted for choosing the wrong way.

Why did people have to run after such fads and phantoms when the Truth was placed clearly before them? Why belittle yourself to worship Elvis Presley, when you could worship Dionysus, the true spring of that force? Why worship Marilyn Monroe, when you could lose yourself in Aphrodite, of whom Monroe was a pale, dim shadow? What did the worship of Jesus Christ offer that wasn't found in the worship of Orpheus? Why worship Odin, when the temples of both Zeus and Hermes were open to you?

It was sheer perversity! It was the decadence of this modern age. People weren't satisfied with the ways that had guided their ancestors. The true worship of the Great Gods no longer *amused* them. It no longer satisfied their jaded, tired, sensation-seeking minds. They must run after anything new, anything frippery and sparkly, that might excite them for a few hours.

And, meanwhile, Mars was failing. How could people find the strength to order and discipline their lives, to take on the difficult but necessary responsibilities of marriage and child-rearing, when they had no strength at their centre, but only a whirl of fad and immorality?

Swinging to face his computer, Zeuslove tapped in a memo.

'Subject: Odinstoy Atkinson, newcomer from Earth. God-speaker for Odin. As much information as possible, please.'

He mailed it to his secretary and all informants.

Landing on Mars

'*Freemen, Freewomen,*' said the Captain's voice over the speakers. '*In a short while, we'll be connecting to the Mars Space-El. Please obey instructions for your safety and comfort.*'

Affie turned to Odinstoy, her mouth open and her eyes wide and shining. Her hair was washed over with cloud-waves of pink and even magenta.

Odinstoy smiled to see her so excited, but almost pitied her too. Affie's mother had deserted her, and her father – before shooting himself – had sold her into bondery yet, despite these shocks, Affie was convinced that everything would be lovely when they reached Mars; that all their wishes would be granted. Odinstoy knew that every gift from Odin had a razor-edge hidden in it; and every wish He granted, He might suddenly withdraw. There was no use raging about it, or weeping, and saying it was unfair. In Odin's world, things were as He made them; and so be it.

'We're here, we're here!' Affie said, her hair flushed almost to scarlet – but waves of indigo suddenly pulsed through it as her excitement swiftly turned to a cold, sick fear. Oh Gods, they were at Mars. Now everything had to begin. Everything strange. Now, instead of merely dreaming, she had to make her dreams come true: become a fashion designer or a make-up artist, become rich. And she had to do it on Mars, which she knew only from the talk on ship; where she knew hardly anyone. And what skills or knowledge did she have?

Odinstoy called Gift to her and stood, taking the little boy's hand. She looked at Affie as she led Gift away, and Affie followed – to the Observation Lounge, as it turned out. Many of the other passengers had gathered there.

The great round of Mars was turned up to them, marbled green, blue and red. Its pattern, half veiled by cloud, changed slowly as they circled it. 'There's Olympus,' someone said, and there was a muted cheer. Affie caught her breath. It was hard to believe that it wasn't a video they were watching, a computer-animation; hard to believe they had really travelled thirty-five million miles and were going to walk on that alien surface. Even though she stood among Martians, who chit-chatted among themselves, she felt her throat close at the thought.

She looked sidelong at Odinstoy. Did Toy understand what an awesome sight they were looking at? Originally, Odinstoy hadn't even known that Mars and Earth were different planets – or known what 'outer space' meant. 'Mars!' Affie whispered to her. 'Mars!'

Odinstoy stared at 'the red planet', which was no longer so red. It was still named for the God of War, though; and Odin, who had brought her here, was a god of war, too. And, true enough, He had brought her to battle. Whatever else Mars was, it would be another battlefield for her.

Gift pulled on her hand and called to her. Stooping over him, pointing at the screen, she said, 'That's where we're going.'

'Mars?' he said.

'Mars.'

'Good old Mars,' Thorsgift said, joining them. He sighed. 'I'll take you out to see Mount Olympus one sol. It's bigger than anything on Earth – it's beautiful. And there – there's the Space-El.'

It was hard to see – a ghost-grey ribbon, delicate as a hair, often fading out of sight except for the red and green lights twinkling on it.

'We'll be docking soon,' Thorsgift said.

An hour later, they still hadn't docked. The Captain kept apologising. Affie couldn't stand it any longer. Circling Mars was too awesome, too frightening and exhausting. She'd looked forward to reaching it for too long, and dreaded it for just as long; and now it seemed like they would never, ever actually set foot on it.

She went back to the lounge, got herself a cup of hot chocolate, and switched on a computer, to amuse herself by trying new hairstyles and clothes on a virtual-self. Many other passengers had gathered in the lounge too. Affie didn't know how long passed: too long – her jaws ached from gritting her teeth, she was getting a headache – before a computerised voice said, '*Passengers*

27

are requested to please find seats and strap themselves in, while we dock.'

Affie was half inclined to ignore the instruction – yet another false alarm – but then everyone else began coming in from Observation, and finding seats, and fastening straps – and they were nearly all Martians, and must know the routine. She saw Odinstoy, Gift and Thorsgift together, and went to join them.

'They're just covering themselves in case someone bumps their head and sues them,' Thorsgift said, as he strapped himself in anyway.

Locking onto the Space-El was no more exciting for the passengers than riding in a taxi, though Affie felt her heart beating faster, and knew that red highlights were flickering through her hair. Her excitement was solely due to her half-fearful, half-thrilled anticipation of what life on Mars was going to be like. She saw that her fellow passengers were all unfastening their belts. The information panel was telling them that they could.

'Now we're locked on,' Thorsgift said, 'it'll take about five sols to get down to the surface.'

'How long in days?' Affie asked. She couldn't think in sols.

'Oh – about four.'

Four days! After thinking that they were about to land on Mars, she had to find something to do with herself for four more days. It was so dull, pacing about the ship, eating cardboard meals, going to bed . . . But after a couple of sols she realised that she was becoming heavier. She felt it in her legs and hips when she took a step, in her back and neck when she stood. It was no longer so easy to leap up and touch the roof.

'It's Mars,' Thorsgift said, when he overheard her mention this to Odinstoy. 'Gravity. The closer we get to the surface, the more you'll feel it.'

'I thought Martian gravity was weak,' Affie said, annoyed that he was hanging around Odinstoy again, and butting into their talk. 'I thought that was why you're all so overgrown.'

'Martian gravity's weaker than Earth's,' Thorsgift said. 'It's a smaller planet. But it's stronger than the ship's gravity.'

'It's the only time I'm glad to put on weight,' said another passenger, a woman. 'It means we're nearly home.'

Home, Affie thought. Would there be a time when she would call Mars 'home' as casually as that?

'*Freemen and Freewomen, I'm happy to inform you that we are now grounded on Mars—*'

There were some cheers and whoops, some a little edgy with relief. Affie and Odinstoy looked at each other. Affie thought she'd never seen a bigger smile on Odinstoy's face.

'*Disembarkation will take some time. Please be patient. Thank you for travelling with us, and enjoy your onward journey. Thank you!*'

'Mars?' Gift said.

Instead of ignoring him, Affie leaned towards him. 'Yes! Mars! I can't wait, can you?'

'Red mice!' Gift said, and Affie answered, 'Red peas!'
'Red cats!'
'Red cows!'
'Red, red, red – everything red!'
Odinstoy said nothing, but smiled to see them getting on together.

People had gathered up their few bits and pieces – no one carried much luggage on interplanet flights – and shuffled through the lounges, crowding at the doors, queueing in the corridors. Affie couldn't shake off the feeling that she was simply arriving at an airport on Earth – arriving in France, or Switzerland – and the whole space-flight had been a dream.

Ahead, she could see the top of a door above people's heads, and hear odd noises, and the Captain's voice saying, 'Thank you – good sol – thank you – good sol . . .' She realised that this was the final door, the exit from the ship that had carried them thirty-five million miles from home. Beyond that doorway was *Mars*. Suddenly, she was very fond of the ship and didn't want to leave it.

She couldn't breathe, there wasn't enough air. There was no air on Mars, she was breathing poison! But it was simply fear. After the long journey that never ended, here was the end. In a moment they were going to see the place where they were to spend the rest of their lives.

Four people in front of her – three – two – 'Thank you! Good sol!' She stepped through the door and—

Mars was grey. It was a dusty, grey hall; a hangar, grey-lit. People were hurrying away from her towards glass doors. She scuttled after them, trying not to feel disappointment. Thorsgift passed her in long strides, hoisting a bag onto his shoulder and saying, 'Home!'

Affie glanced back and saw that Odinstoy and Gift were behind her, with other passengers. She went back to join them, and felt slightly better for being with them. They should stick close together. They only had each other.

Beyond the dusty glass doors was a beige room. A row of booths were strung across it, and people were queueing at them.

Affie stopped. Entry control.

Odinstoy and Gift, swinging their linked hands, were chanting between them:

'Red peas!'

'Red mice!'

'Red cats!'

'Red custard!'

Affie nudged Odinstoy sharply and nodded towards the booths. Odinstoy looked at them indifferently. 'Odin is with us.' Leading Gift, she walked on.

Affie stayed where she was, feeling a great weight descend from the base of her throat into her belly. Breathing was harder. She forced herself on, trying not to let her steps slow as she drew near the booths, but couldn't help it. They had been doubted on Earth – what if orders to arrest them had been sent ahead?

Thorsgift looked into the scanner, spoke briefly to the Martian in the booth, and passed through. Odinstoy was next, and she smiled at the man on duty, and lifted Gift so he could look into the scanner. Setting the child down, she looked into the scanner herself, without any sign of nerves. The man in the booth spoke to her, and she smiled and answered, as if it was easy. Affie, watching as her heart thudded, admired her calmness, but knew that Odinstoy had a determination that could carry anything off. Affie felt herself to be far weaker.

Odinstoy was waved through the gate, and Affie was alone. She wanted to run back to the safety of the ship, but her legs moved her forward.

She smiled at the Martian security man, feeling the smile freeze her face – surely it looked false and suspicious? Then she looked into the scanner while voices screamed in her head: They're going to know, they're going to know!

'Thank you, Freewoman,' the man said. 'Have you brought any food or drink from Earth?'

'No!'

'Any plants, or rocks or soil?'

'No,' she answered, more calmly.

'Thank you, Freewoman. Have a good sol.'

She tottered after Odinstoy on shaky legs. Bob Sing's work had held: the database said her iris-scan matched that of someone called Freya Atkinson.

Now she was in Arrivals and, drawing a deep breath, looking round for her first real sight of Mars.

The Arrivals Hall – well, it was hardly a hall, not like the one on Earth. It was small, shabby and dated. The colours, the adverts on the walls, the patterns on the tip-up seats – it was all just far enough out of date to set her teeth on edge in that irritating way. Is all of Mars like this? Affie thought.

And the people: the arrivals, and the people who'd come to meet them. They were all lanky and pale, and their clothes and their hair were out of date, and the men were all bearded . . . Shocking. What were they thinking? At least there would be scope for someone who *knew* about clothes and hair and make-up.

Thorsgift said to Odinstoy, 'You'll be OK with Rebecca. She'll see you all right – I'll just go and see if I can find—' And he darted away, leaving them in the middle of the Arrivals Hall by themselves.

A small knot of tall Martians, both men and women, came towards them in a determined way, smiling and holding out their hands. In the lead were an elderly man and woman who hadn't done anything about their greying hair and wrinkles. A step behind them came a younger couple and, behind them, a bonder. Affie knew she was a bonder straight away, because she hung back, had cropped hair, and was dressed so badly.

Odinstoy watched them come too. She'd known, even before Thorsgift had mentioned Rebecca, that the small group weren't just moving in their general direction, but were coming to meet them. Dropping her son's hand, she went towards them.

The elderly couple smiled and held out their hands – and Affie saw the smiles drop from their faces as Odinstoy walked straight past them, straight past the second couple, and embraced the startled bonder behind them. Affie was as shocked as the Martians. What was Odinstoy *doing*? Did she think this was a good start to the life they had to make on Mars?

'Good health, good life!' Odinstoy said. 'I love you, sweetheart! What's your name? I am Odinstoy.'

The bonder's face, as Odinstoy released her, was a confusion of shock, bewilderment, fright and pleasure. 'Dora! My name's Dora . . . Sorry, sorry—' This to her owners, who had turned and were staring.

'I am so pleased to meet you, Dora,' Odinstoy said, and then turned with a big smile to the older woman. 'Rebecca! I am so glad to meet you!' She held out her arms for an embrace.

Rebecca, flustered at being addressed by name, hesitated, but then went into Odinstoy's arms and returned her hug. 'Welcome to Mars! We can't say how delighted – and honoured – and pleased – we are to meet you at last!'

'And so say all of us!' said the old man. There was a murmuring and muttering of agreement from the others. They seemed prepared to overlook that she'd greeted their bonder before them.

'My husband, Heimdal,' Rebecca said, as she stepped back from Odinstoy – who immediately embraced Heimdal and kissed his cheek.

'There is love for you,' she said.

The younger couple then came forward eagerly for their hugs. 'My daughter, Bergthora,' Rebecca said proudly, 'and her husband, Hart.'

'And this,' Odinstoy said, holding out a hand to call him to her, 'is my son, Odinsgift.' The little boy ran into the centre of the little group of people and leaned against Odinstoy's legs. The tall Martians all looked down at him.

'Oh, aren't you sweet?' Rebecca said.

'He'll break some hearts when he grows up,' Heimdal said.

'And my wife, Affie.'

Affie went to join them, a little piqued at having been introduced after Odinsgift. The Martians were all so tall that standing in the middle of them was like standing at the bottom of a deep well. Their clothes were of very good quality, she noticed, and the women's jewellery too, though it was small and simple. They had money, then – so why didn't they look after their faces?

It was funny to see the expressions on those faces as they looked at her. She saw the quick lift of eyebrows from the men, as they recognised a more-than-usually pretty girl, and the shock and bafflement on all the faces as they heard that she was Odinstoy's wife. Some of them must have heard the broadcast from the ship, but perhaps they'd been hoping it was mistaken. However, those expressions were quickly covered by smiles. God-speakers were not ordinary people. Odinstoy was favoured by Odin, and if she wanted a sister and wife combined in one person, then Odin be praised! They turned to Affie, smiling, stooping, holding out their hands.

'So pleased to meet you.'

'Such a pleasure to welcome you—'

'We hope – we *know* – that you're all going to be very happy—'

It was very nice to be treated with such politeness and respect again. Affie tossed her hair, to set it rippling, so the orange cloud-shapes of pure pleasure would be seen to advantage.

Thorsgift came over, bringing his family with him – parents, a sister, even grandparents, all of them very tall. They all greeted Odinstoy too, with ducking heads, and smiles, and another outpouring of names, all of which seemed to start with 'Thor', whether they were men or women. Thorsgift apologised for going off and leaving them: '. . . but it's been so long since I've seen my folks. Anyway, I know Rebecca will take good care of you. But I'll come and call – tomorrow? Can I call on you tomorrow?'

Odinsgift embraced him, and kissed him when he lowered his head. 'You are always welcome, Thorsgift. "No greater riches than a friend."'

Thorsgift was a little surprised at such a warm parting, but pleased too.

'We'll look after them,' Rebecca said. 'Off you go.' When Thorsgift walked away, she said, 'Well now! What we plan to do with you, if it's all right, is to put you up in a hotel for tonight –'

A hotel! Affie thought, and dreamed of the luxury she was entitled to.

'– and then, tomorrow, there are a lot of details to sort out: your IDs and tax details and all that—'

'We'll help you with all that,' said Bergthora kindly, stooping over them.

'And Mars television would rather like to interview you, if that's all right.'

'Television!' Affie said. 'Oh yes, Toy, you have to!'

'I would be happy to speak to them,' Odinstoy said.

'I tried to put them off until tomorrow,' Rebecca said, looking guilty. 'I really did. But they were very insistent. Do you think you could bear to speak to them today?'

'Oh yes!' Affie said. 'No problem at all!'

'Then there's tonight,' said Heimdal. 'It's entirely up to you. We can take you out to dinner, and show you something of the city – or you can have a quiet night at your hotel.'

Before Affie could speak, Odinstoy said, 'The quiet night.'

'Of course!' Rebecca said. 'You'll want to draw breath and take stock, so to speak. Have a cup of tea. Well! – This way. We'll catch the mono . . .' And with a wave of her arm, she ushered them towards the glass doors.

As she and Odinstoy followed the Martians, Affie felt a weird, light-headed sense of surreality, as if all she saw was not real, but only reflections on glass, glimpsed at an angle; and all she heard was only the garbled mishearing of some half-understood lyric. Three months of travel, thirty-five million miles, and now: 'Oh, let's go and have a cup of tea.'

What did you think landing on Mars would be like? she asked herself. What else could it be like? Every journey, however long, had to end at some time. And then – you had a cup of tea.

She noticed that both Freewomen were staring at her hair. The men were too, though they were trying harder to hide it. And she was drawing long stares from others not even of their party. Of course, Affie thought, they've never seen anyone like me. She only had to glance round to know that she was easily the most beautiful person in the building. And, since she was feeling apprehensive but excited, the colours in her hair would be shifting through blue and lilac to pale pink.

'You have lovely hair,' Bergthora said.

'Thank you. I was designed.'

'The Gods be praised!' Rebecca said, and the others looked surprised and, Affie thought, impressed. Designing couldn't be common on Mars. It made her feel good to know it.

Doors slid open and let them into an area of paved walkways, with plants in tubs and troughs. There were balconies, from which they could look down a long way to streets between buildings. There were vehicles moving down there. Disembarking from the Space-El had evidently brought them into the topmost floor of a tall building.

'Look up,' Rebecca said, pointing upwards.

Odinstoy and Affie looked up and saw a roof above them, made of huge hexagon shapes, each hexagon bigger than a house. All of them held a bubble that glinted with rainbow colours. The sky above the roof, seen through the hexagonal bubbles, was a soft, milky pink-mauve.

The bubbles flexed and moved, changing colours slightly as they did so. And there was a noise. Louder than the sound of feet on pavements, and wheels and chatter, and the clatter of luggage on trolleys – louder than this was a creaking and groaning, a booming, like wind, a thudding.

'Our domes,' Rebecca said. 'You'll have to grow to love them. They're everywhere.'

'There's a storm going on out there,' Hart said. 'It's been blowing for three days. That's what's making all the noise.'

'The domes are trying to lift off!' Heimdal said, with a laugh, as he led the way along a walkway. 'Don't worry – they won't. They've seen us through worse than this.'

Still looking up as he walked, Hart said, 'The maintenance crews'll be busy.'

'They still let us come down the Space-El!' Affie said, wondering if she'd been in danger as she imagined that fragile thread being tossed about by storms.

'Oh, they don't often close the El,' Hart said. 'Anyway, most of it wouldn't be bothered by surface storms.'

The bonder led them through a door into a tiled, echoing hall where people hurried to and fro, and there were gates, and machines on the walls, and noise. Heimdal and Rebecca stood still, and the others gathered round them – but the bonder went off by herself to one of the machines on the wall. 'She's gone to buy your tickets,' Rebecca said.

She'd hardly closed her mouth before Odinstoy walked away and went to join the bonder at the machine. Affie could see that all the Martians were taken aback by this and embarrassed. Rebecca smiled brightly at her, determined not to notice how odd Odinstoy was being. Affie thought of reminding them that Odinstoy had been born a bonder, but instead said, 'Shall we be staying in the Space-El hotel? There must be one, I imagine . . .'

'Oh no, we've booked you into the Hotel Ares,' Rebecca said, her eyes straying to where Odinstoy was returning with the bonder. 'It's more central – and much nicer.'

'There's so much industry round the El,' Bergthora said. 'Not a nice area, really – though the hotel is, of course. But—'

'All together again!' Rebecca said, as Odinstoy and the bonder rejoined them, and led the way onwards. The Martians showed their phones to the gate, but Affie, Odinstoy and Gift had to present it with their plastic tickets. It opened to allow them through, and they followed Rebecca through echoing corridors to a tiled platform, where they boarded a long cylinder. There were long, bench-like seats, on which they were all able to sit together, except the bonder, who stood beside them, hanging onto a strap.

There was a great hissing as the doors closed, and the mono sped forward and emerged from the station into the air. Affie exclaimed with delight, and with a little fear. They were above all the buildings, and could see just how huge the arch of the dome was; and, above them, they were closer to its structure of hexagons and bubbles, with their shifting rainbow lights. Maintenance trackways traced across it, black against the light, interrupted with square platforms. As the mono neared the wall of the dome, the hexagon frames looming larger, they could glimpse other domes, and half-domes, and three-quarter-domes attached to the one they were in, seeming to lean on it.

'Oh! Are we—?' Affie clapped her hand to her mouth in alarm, fearing that they were going to hit the wall of the dome, but then they were outside it, and speeding through the open Mars air towards another dome.

All the Martians laughed at her, except the bonder.

'There's a door it goes through,' Heimdal said. 'It doesn't open until the mono touches it, and seals behind it – there's hardly any exchange of atmospheres.'

'Take a good look,' Hart said. 'You won't see much of Mars without the domes in the way.'

Affie and Odinstoy twisted to look out of the windows, and Odinstoy called Gift's attention to it.

The sky, between clouds, was not quite blue: a pretty colour, Affie thought.

The dome was surrounded by forests of greenery, all moving in a breeze: every kind of green, touched with gold and russet and spreading off, apparently unbroken to the horizon.

'Our regolith is very fertile,' Heimdal said.

'Your – what?' Affie asked.

'Regolith,' Hart said. '"Soil" you'd call it. And the air's rich in carbon dioxide – that helps.'

'Plant a bread roll here,' Heimdal said, 'and it grows into a bread-roll tree.'

Did it? Affie wondered, picturing a tree hung with little rolls covered in black poppy-seeds. Had there been some genetic designing done with *trees*?

Heimdal laughed at her face.

'He's joking you, my dear,' Rebecca said. 'It's an old, *old* joke!'

'The best kind,' Heimdal said. He twisted in his seat. 'And behind you is our industry.'

Through the windows on the other side of the mono-car, they saw the domes rising above them and, protrud-ing through the domes, tall chimneys, from which streamed plumes of smoke and vapour: black, grey, yellow, orange.

'We make a lot of steel,' Hart said. 'We bring the ore in from the asteroids.'

Odinstoy looked at Affie, as if hopeful she could explain, but it was almost as meaningless to her. And Affie didn't *want* to understand; she didn't want to be told about these strange little snippets she could see through the windows, as if she could take in Mars within a few minutes of arriving. It was all too much. She suddenly felt that she simply wanted to be at the hotel, in a room as much like any other hotel room as possible, and sleep.

'The chimneys go up out of the domes,' Heimdal went on relentlessly, smiling, 'so they can release pollution into the atmosphere!' He seemed to think this a good joke, but Odinstoy turned on him her most intent, blank stare. Affie glanced at Rebecca, trying to find some clue. He was puzzled by their lack of understanding. 'Pollution's a big deal on Earth, isn't it? You don't have pollution on Earth any more, do you? Isn't that right?'

Odinstoy leaned back in her seat, settling Gift's head into her shoulder, and closed her eyes. Affie saw that she was going to have to make polite conversation, but didn't know what she ought to say. She'd never given pollution, or lack of it, a thought.

'You cleaned it all up,' Heimdal said. 'Well, we *like* pollution! We *want* pollution! You know why?'

'Because you're mad?' Affie guessed.

Everyone laughed, except Odinstoy and the bonder. Gift laughed because the people around him did. 'Oh, she's a one!' Heimdal said. 'No – we *are* mad, but that's not why. We're still terraforming. We *need* pollution – it's helping to raise temperatures, create atmosphere—'

'How interesting,' Affie said.

'Heim, they're tired,' Rebecca said. 'They just want to relax until we get to the hotel.'

The mono-car seemed about to crash into a dome again, but shot through a door into a station, which had been built into the top storey of a tall building. People got on and got off, and then the car moved on, emerging from the station to travel on its rail near the roof of the immense dome. Rebecca pointed down and said, 'There's the cathedral of Mars.'

Affie leaned to see. She didn't know what to expect of a Martian cathedral. But she was disappointed again – it was much like one on Earth: very big, built of white, shining stone, with columns and porticos and statues of Zeus.

Heimdal said, 'The Earth party at prayer.'

Rebecca shushed him.

'Well, they might as well know what's what!' he said. 'You can bet the C of M's already found out everything about them.'

'About us? Me?' Affie said, with a mixture of surprise and fright. She couldn't imagine why the Church of Mars would want to know about her – but, since she was a runaway bonder and an imposter, it was alarming to think that anyone might ask questions.

'About Odinstoy, dear, not you,' Rebecca said.

'About both of them,' Heimdal said. 'They're together, aren't they?'

That wasn't reassuring. Affie looked at Odinstoy, who returned her gaze quite calmly, making Affie feel angry. 'Why would they ask questions about Odinstoy?'

'Because she speaks for Odin,' Heimdal said, as if it was obvious. 'They keep tabs on all of us.'

'He exaggerates,' Rebecca said. 'If you don't worship the – the *established* Gods, people are a little suspicious of you sometimes, that's all.'

'Ha!' Heimdal said. 'I tell you, both of you, remember this: "The people of Mars are free, but some are more free than others."'

'Yes,' Odinstoy said, startling them because it had been so long since she'd spoken. They all looked at her expectantly. 'Some of you are more free than your bonders.'

There was an embarrassed silence. Everyone looked out of the windows or at the floor. Then Rebecca cleared her throat. 'He does go on,' she said. 'It's not as bad as he makes out, honestly. Oh – here's our station!' She spoke with relief.

Aliens

'We're aliens on Mars,' Affie said, looking at the card in her hand. It held all the information about her, as faked by Odinstoy's friend: her name, her medical details, a blank for her employment history . . . Everything. A lot of it was true. Bob Sing had only tweaked things here and there. He'd left out entirely, for instance, the fact that she had been bonded.

The Martian authorities had added the date of her arrival, and a category – resident alien – and given her an ID number, which entitled her to services, and to be taxed. Odinstoy and Gift had cards too.

Affie grinned, kicked her legs out straight as she sat on the edge of the bed, and looked round the hotel room.

It was nothing special. There were two neat beds and a cot for Gift; there was a desk and a computer; a wardrobe and lamps, a kettle, a small fridge and a snack machine – just an ordinary, inexpensive hotel room, pleasantly decorated. But when Rebecca had led them from the monostation into the foyer, Affie had given a happy gasp. A wide expanse of marble had shone before them in the light falling through glass. There had been white columns decorated with gilding, and a fountain, whose centrepiece was a gleaming bronze sculpture of breastplate, helmet and spear, representing the God, Ares. It was old-fashioned, yes, and the sort of décor which, when perpetrated by her stepmother, Affie had described as, 'Dull, dull, dull,' but now it spoke to her of wealth, and all the security and comfort that wealth could wrap her in. She had missed it.

And even though their room was plain, she could imagine that somewhere above their heads were splendid suites, with many rooms and sunken baths, with gorgeous draperies and access to a lamplit roof-garden – except there couldn't be a roof-garden under a dome, could there?

Whatever – the luxury to which she was born and entitled was nearby, and would be hers again. It would, she was determined it would.

This afternoon they were to be interviewed by a television crew! That was a step in the right direction. Fame – then fortune.

'Be careful what you say to the television people,' she said to Odinstoy, who was lying on the other bed with Gift, holding him as he slept. Brat, Affie thought, slightly nettled, as usual, by the attention Odinstoy paid him. 'I mean it. Be careful.'

Odinstoy smiled. 'I shall say what I shall say.'

'Don't say anything dreadful,' Affie begged. 'Take it seriously. Rebecca said the interviewer is really well known here; everyone will be watching. You've got to sell yourself. If you make a bad impression—'

'I speak for Odin.'

'Well, *don't*. *He's* bound to say something dreadful.'

Odinstoy gave her a long, hard look with those intense, dark eyes, and Affie thought she was going to be told off – but then Odinstoy relaxed, and smiled. 'Me and Odin – we'll be good.'

And so you should, Affie thought. They'd risked enough to get to Mars. Why harm their chances now? She looked at her watch and, as she did so, there was a knock at the door, making her jump. She looked at Odinstoy, who looked back and smiled.

'I'm not a bonder any more,' she said.

'Neither am I!' said Affie. But now it was a matter, not of bonder and free, but of who had the strongest will. It was Odinstoy. When the door was rapped again, Affie got up and answered it.

Rebecca was standing outside in the corridor and slightly behind her was a man – a tall man, even for a Martian and, for a Martian, most unusually tanned.

'Oh Affie,' Rebecca said, 'are you ready? The television people—'

The tall man leaned past Rebecca, holding out his hand. 'I'm a television person, Affie – *so* pleased to meet you.'

He had a most kindly, pleasing face – pleasing rather than handsome – and a large white smile. His suit, she saw, looked expensive, and so was his watch. She liked him even before he said, 'That hair! Lovely! That face! My stars, you *are* a beauty, aren't you?'

There opened before Affie dreams of a career in television.

'And this is Odinstoy!' said the man.

Odinstoy had come to stand behind Affie.

The man stepped into the room, making Affie move aside. 'Odinstoy,' the man said, stooping almost double in order to take both of Odinstoy's hands. 'I'm honoured to welcome you to Mars. I'm sure you're going to inspire and invigorate us.'

Odinstoy looked back at him calmly.

'I'm Leander Fitzpatrick . . .' He left a slight pause, as if he expected her to know his name and react. Her stare remained calm and impassive.

'Oh, everyone knows our Leander,' Rebecca said.

'You're too kind,' he said.

'Every night he's there, giving us all the gossip, keeping us all in touch.'

'I do love gossip,' he said. 'But, Odinstoy – I may call you that, mayn't I? – I'm so delighted, I'm truly honoured to be interviewing you for my show. Thank you so much for agreeing.'

'Odin told me to,' Odinstoy said.

'Well, thank Odin! Now, my camera's scouting out a suitable place downstairs, but if we could just run through a few things? A wee rehearsal, if you like . . .'

Odinstoy just shrugged and went back to the bed, where Gift was waking up. Being a bonder, of course, she had no idea how to behave. Affie said, 'Come in! Sit down! Would you like a drink?' She was glad to be able to take part in the scene. After that first wonderful mention of her face and hair, she'd felt rather overshadowed by Odinstoy.

Leander Fitzpatrick came in, and folded his great length into the easy chair, while Rebecca took the hard chair by the desk. 'I won't have anything, thanks – working.' He leaned forward in his chair, looking at Odinsgift. 'Who is this little charmer?'

Gift became shy, and hid his face against Odinstoy, who said, 'My son.'

'Our son,' Affie corrected, unwilling to be left out.

'We often do bits on newcomers,' Leander said. 'We're still quite a small community, you know, still quite a village mentality. We like to know who's who. So, Odinstoy, you were a bonder on Earth?'

'You're going to say that?' Affie said.

'I'm still bonded,' Odinstoy said. 'I belong to Odin.'

'Really?' Leander said. 'Oh, I think we'll mention that! And you two are married? That'll go down well. Marriage, commitment, children, passing on the heritage – that's what we like!'

'And when are you yourself going to marry, Leander?' Rebecca asked.

'Oh, that question again!' he said, and laughed. 'Tomorrow, if you'll run away with me, dear lady! Shall we go down and see if we can get it wrapped?'

They all trooped down the corridor to the lift, Gift hand in hand with Odinstoy, and the others following behind. The lift delivered them to the more public part of the hotel: all white walls and gilding. Affie's heart lifted, and a determination came over her to be in front of the camera with Odinstoy, not pushed aside as a little wifey. She had to make herself known, make an impression, if she was to make something of herself here on Mars.

The 'camera' was a bearded man, dressed all in black. Affie knew at once that he was a bonder. He'd chosen the hotel's almost empty restaurant as the spot for the interview. He wanted Odinstoy to sit at a table in front of a gilded relief of Ares' shield, spear and helmet. Affie pulled up a chair and sat beside her, leaning close.

'No,' the camera said. 'Not you.'

'Oh yes,' said Leander. 'She's gorgeous, can't waste her. The little boy too. He's so pretty.' He leaned back, sighed, and framed them with his hands. 'You're such a picture, such a pretty little family.'

The interview wasn't how Affie had imagined it. She'd thought there would be lots of lights and cables and make-up people, and a director shouting instructions. Instead there was just the empty restaurant, and the camera held on the bonder's shoulder. Leander stood to one side and asked them questions, while they talked to the camera. If they forgot, and looked at him, he would point at the camera, and then, sometimes, repeat the question. 'Are you enjoying Mars?' he asked.

Affie jumped in with the answer, a big smile, and a shake of her hair. 'Oh yes! We haven't seen much of it yet, but we're so much looking forward to seeing more . . .'

'Tell us a little about how you decided to come to Mars.'

'Oh! Well! My husband – Odinstoy – was appointed God-speaker to Odin here, and so . . .'

Odinstoy hardly spoke, but only held Gift and watched Affie as she chattered. But that was fair enough, Leander thought. Affie was charming, and Odinstoy looked as dark, mysterious and brooding as a speaker for Odin should look.

'That's fine,' he said, and the cameraman relaxed. 'Thank you to you both. When will you be speaking first, Odinstoy? For Odin, I mean. I'd certainly like to be there with the camera.'

Odinstoy and Affie looked at each other.

'We don't know that yet,' said Affie. 'But we'll be sure to let you know.'

'But that's business,' Leander said, clapping his hands. 'Turning to more important stuff – pleasure, my pleasure – I'd love to have you along to one of my dinner parties, sweethearts.'

'We'd love to come!' Affie cried.

'Then I shall certainly be in touch.' He shook hands with them all, even Gift, and kissed them on the cheek too, but it was clear that they were now expected to leave. They went out into the foyer, where Rebecca was waiting for them, and peered back into the restaurant, to see Leander seat himself in an armchair, and ask all the same questions he'd asked them, while the camera filmed him.

'We'll all look forward to seeing you on the telly,' Rebecca said, as they crossed the foyer, passing the fountain that splashed and tinkled over Ares' armour. 'Isn't it exciting?'

At Home

Their taxi had driven a long way from the city of Ares, through forests and tall cornfields, before the cluster of domes enclosing the village of Osbourne rose up ahead of them. Some of the domes were almost complete hemi-spheres; others were segmented, added on to the larger domes to extend them in one direction or another. They were all built of the straight-sided cells, as if constructed by gigantic bees, and each cell held its transparent bubble, scattering the light into rainbows. Emerging from the vast fields of tall crops, with the pink-blue sky above, the canton's domes were strange. Affie couldn't decide if they were ugly or beautiful.

She peered from the car windows with a new interest, hoping that their house wasn't going to be in one of those barrack-like blocks they'd passed on the edge of the city of Ares, but Osbourne was different. The domes of Ares had been filled with buildings, rising high in towers and blocks, with mono-stations on their upper storeys, and mono-rails suspended in the air. The domes of Osbourne weren't as big, and the buildings weren't as high. They all seemed quite pretty, with window-boxes and hanging baskets dripping with flowers of all colours. And it was, indeed, in front of one of these pretty buildings with balconies that the car stopped. Please, please, Affie thought, don't let them take us round the back to some shed.

Instead, once the bonder had opened the car door for them, they were taken up a path lined with flowering bushes, Heimdal hurrying ahead to open the door by looking into its scanner. 'We'll get that set up to recognise you before we leave.'

Odinstoy, carrying Gift in her arms, stopped just by the door near a bush of blue flowers, looked round and, with Gift's cheek resting against hers, smiled. And all of them gazed at her and smiled back at the young mother, dressed as a man, holding her child.

'Would you like to go in?' Rebecca asked, almost in a whisper.

Odinstoy nodded slightly and carried Gift into the house. They all stood back and let her go first, even Affie.

How does she do it? Affie wondered. How does she get everyone to just – to just *bow* to her? She's only a bonder, really.

Affie pressed forward, so that she entered the house behind Odinstoy. Rebecca and Heimdal followed them, but the others stayed outside because, as Affie quickly realised, there wasn't room.

The place was tiny. The door let them straight into the main room. The floor was tiled with large, smooth square flagstones in a dark red. A light-green rug lay over them. A rather grubby, thin, worn green rug. A rug that had already been well used by strangers. Affie didn't like that.

A steel ladder caught Affie's eye. It led up – and Affie realised that what at first glance she had taken for a beamed ceiling was, in fact, the underside of a large bed. A pot of green, leafy plants hung from it. The window was tall, to light both the space under, and the space above, the bed.

In the space under the bed, a long padded bench ran along two walls, making an L-shaped sitting area with a low table in front of it. A viewing screen was built into the wall.

Behind the benches, the walls were panelled, but Rebecca opened the panels. They were cupboards. 'Plenty of space for clothes and things.'

Plenty of space? Was she joking? It wasn't even as big, or as nice, as the hotel room in Ares.

'Plenty of shelves,' Rebecca said, and there were lots of recesses and shelves in the walls.

'Underfloor heating,' Heimdal said. 'Scoot up that ladder and have a look.'

Odinstoy smiled at Affie, and Affie rather slowly climbed the ladder – she didn't scoot. The bed-space was big enough for two, and there were more cupboards and recesses in the walls up here. As she climbed back down, Rebecca was saying, 'The benches convert into beds too.'

Not what *I* would call a bed, Affie thought.

The kitchen was through a sliding door on one side of the room – a long galley, with oven, fridge, and sonic washer all built into the walls, along with cupboards. A little table folded down from one wall. Racks, for more storage, could be hoisted overhead.

The shower room opened on the other side of the main room. There were 'the usual facilities', and a sonic shower, and a sonic hand-washer, but no bath.

'Get your ancestor tree set up,' Heimdal said, 'and you'll be really snug here.' He and Rebecca looked at them expectantly.

'We will be happy here,' Odinstoy said. Her ancestor string was tied around her wrist but, for once, she kept quiet about it. 'Odin will bless you for your care and kindness.'

They were so pleased, they almost wriggled.

Where do the people with money live? Affie thought. Where are the *good* places? Leander Fitzpatrick didn't live in a hutch like this, she would bet.

'We've tried to think of everything you'll need,' Rebecca said, keen to show just how kind and careful they'd been. 'There are clothes in the cupboards – just to help out until you can get stuff of your own. And food in the cupboards, just basics. Our address is on the computer. Just mail if you need anything . . .'

'Odin will bless you,' Odinstoy said.

'We didn't get you a bonder,' Heimdal said. 'We thought you'd want to choose your own.'

'Yes, it's a very personal—' Rebecca began.

Odinstoy said, 'We'll have no bonder.'

Affie turned her head sharply to look at her. The others stared in silence.

'No bonder?' Rebecca said.

'No bonder.' Odinstoy spoke flatly, emphatically. She frowned.

'We'd better leave them to themselves,' Heimdal said.

'Yes, yes, we'll leave you to catch your breaths . . .'

Odinstoy went with them to the door, and said to those who had waited outside, 'Thank you all for your kindness and thoughtfulness. Odin blesses you for it. He will hold you in His hand.'

Then they went away, and they were alone. Affie couldn't quite fit the fact into her mind. They were on Mars. In their new house. This was it: their new life. And it was *shoddy*.

Affie sat down on one of the benches. Odinstoy made coffee in the kitchen, and then wandered about opening cupboards, looking at the clothes hung in them, trying out the viewing screen. Gift, who had been subdued in the presence of strangers, now began to run from the kitchen to the bathroom, and to climb up and down the ladder to the bed-space. Affie could see that living with him, here, in this tiny space, was going to be torture. And there wasn't even going to be a bonder to keep him from annoying them for a few hours.

'Set up your ancestor tree,' Odinstoy said.

'I don't want to.'

'Set it up – people will wonder why you haven't.'

Affie stood, clenching her fists at her sides. 'Is *this* what we came all this way for? Three miserable months! Left Earth? To come to – *this*? It's a kennel! No! I wouldn't keep a dog in here! And we're not going to have a bonder? Ever?'

Odinstoy came over to her, probably meaning to calm her, which enraged Affie.

'If I'd known – this! – I wouldn't have come. They could have given us somewhere decent to live – instead of this hole! And I want a bonder! You didn't ask *me*, did you? *I* want a bonder!'

Without warning, without any change of expression, Odinstoy shoved her, hard. Affie staggered and tried to save herself, but there was nothing to grab. She went over backwards onto the bench, cracking her head against the wall. It hurt horribly.

Clutching her head, wincing, tears filling her eyes, she looked up at Odinstoy standing over her, face expressionless. Affie was scared. Odinstoy was a bonder, she remembered – trained to serve and obey at one time, yes, but underneath that, uneducated, rough, with a grudge against everyone. Dangerous. And I'm trapped alone with her. On Mars.

'Stop whining,' Odinstoy said, and her voice, her words, cut through Affie. She spoke without anger, but with a conviction that was the more authoritative and frightening. 'What would you have stayed on Earth for? To be a bonder? You? You can't wipe your own arse.'

Affie cringed at the crudity.

'You wouldn't have lasted. Another year, and you'd have chucked yourself off the roof. This place? It's a palace. Because it's mine. I've got Gift with me. Mine. Odin sent me here. Mine. If you bugger this up, I'll kill you.'

Odinstoy's long, Japanese eyes held hers, and Affie wanted to be small, to hide. Maybe she wouldn't kill her, but there was no doubt that Odinstoy could and would do her harm. And maybe *would* kill her. Who knew, with a bonder?

'Did you enjoy being a bonder?' Odinstoy said.

Carefully, clutching at her head, Affie sat up. Why ask her that? What did that have to do with anything?

'Did you enjoy being a bonder?'

'I hated it! You know I did!'

'Then why do you want a bonder?'

'Because – everyone else will have one!'

'We won't,' Odinstoy said. 'I shall never own a bonder.'

'But *we'll* have to do everything!'

'Good.'

'But Odinstoy . . . What's the point of being free if you don't have any bonders and you've got to do everything yourself? That's like *being* a bonder.' Odinstoy frowned, and Affie quickly tried another slant. 'We'd be kind to our bonders – because we know what it's like!'

Odinstoy looked down at her with an angry disgust that Affie found as hard to understand as she did to bear. 'What?' Affie cried, not knowing what she'd done.

'You can never be free if you own somebody else,' Odinstoy said – which was just nonsense, the sort of thing people said when they wanted to sound wise and mysterious. But Affie dared not argue any more. She didn't want Odinstoy to attack her again.

'All right. All right. We won't have any bonders.' But I

shall, though, she thought: one day. When I'm not 'married' to you any more. The thought took her by surprise.

Odinstoy offered her hand, pulled Affie up and hugged her, even soothed the back of her head where it had cracked against the wall. 'Be happy,' she said.

Happy? Affie thought. When I'll be doing all the work? While living in this *box*?

'And set up your ancestor tree.'

Affie's first night in their new home was not happy. She did take out her ancestor tree, and plugged it into one of the computer's ports, but it made her feel worse. It was so obviously made for a bigger, wealthier place, and it reminded her of when she'd had a better life. She wanted to put it away in one of the cupboards, but was frightened of starting an argument with Odinstoy.

Later, Odinstoy climbed up into the bed-space with Gift. Affie had unfolded one of the benches, and made it up with sheets from the cupboards and a duvet, resenting having to do it with every little movement. She was supposed to be free now, but she was still doing bonders' work. It wasn't as if she could look forward to having a bonder to do it for her in a few days' time.

Resentment and fear and curiosity kept her awake. She wondered how Odinstoy and Gift were sleeping above her – Gift was quiet, at least. Was Odinstoy lying awake, worrying, as she was? She could have called out and asked, but she refused to do it. And, if Odinstoy was awake, she said nothing.

The bed was probably far more comfortable than the bench she was sleeping on – and Odinstoy hadn't minded making the bed for herself and Gift because she *was* a bonder, really.

What was the point of coming all the way to Mars, to live like a poor person?

But, said that annoyingly reasonable voice at the back of her mind, if you'd stayed on Earth, you'd still have been drudging for the Perrys. Odinstoy saved you from that. You should be grateful. At least, here, you're only working for yourself.

Well, I'm *not* grateful, said Affie's voice, in Affie's head. I *won't* be grateful.

And after all, what was going to happen to them here? What were they supposed to do tomorrow, when they got up? What if no one liked them? What if no one liked Odinstoy's God-speaking? What would they do then? How would they eat? How would they live?

She didn't sleep for a single moment. She wished she'd stayed on Earth, even if it did mean drudging as a bonder.

Gift, of course, woke early, climbed down the ladder and started scampering about, shrieking. He came and peered at Affie, and laughed. She wanted to hit him, but didn't dare.

Odinstoy came down soon after, and Affie got up then. 'Go and wash,' Odinstoy said. 'I'll make breakfast.'

When Affie came out of the shower room, Odinstoy had made a breakfast of eggs and bacon, toast and coffee. She left Affie eating, while she took Gift into the shower room with her. Affie sat at the little fold-down table in the kitchen, eating in a glowering temper. Why did Odinstoy have to be so good at everything, making beds and cooking and minding brats? And so smug with it. She was only a bloody bonder.

Odinstoy and Gift were still eating, and Affie was sprawled on her bed, when the visitors started arriving. Thorsgift came first, bringing flowers and a jar of honey from his mother's bees – but he'd hardly said hello when other people came. Women, mostly. They brought presents of pies and cakes, and flasks of home-made wine and beer. In they crowded, cramming themselves onto the benches, even sitting on the ladder that led up to the bed. A couple of them took it on themselves to make up the beds, chivvying Affie out of the way while they did so, and others cleared the breakfast things, and put them through the sonic washer. They all wanted to introduce themselves to Odinstoy, jabbering out a long string of names: Thoras and Freyas and Ingas and Wulfrunas, with the occasional Jane or Venus. They all fawned over Odinstoy and Gift, trying to ingratiate themselves, but despite that, Affie was considerably cheered by their presence. They admired her ancestor tree, for one thing, and looked at the pictures, and cooed over its prettiness.

'Real silver!'

'Beautifully made!'

'How many generations?'

'Oh, about thirty-five, I think,' Affie said, and enjoyed the way they looked at each other, so impressed.

Her stepmother, back on Earth, had once said that most of the Millington ancestors were invented, but Minerva wasn't here to be spiteful.

'Not many people have so many,' one of the Thoras or Ingas said.

'Here are mine,' Odinstoy said, and held up her wrist, with her ancestor string tied round it. They drew another kind of admiration, and Odinstoy told off her bead, locket, medallion and bit of stone while they crowded round her. Affie was tempted to display some of her ancestors, but then thought about some of the awkward questions that might be asked about her father . . . Better not.

Still, the company, the chatter and laughter did a lot to lift her mood, and the visitors also did the boring house-work. If they were going to do that every day, then they wouldn't need a bonder. Maybe Mars wouldn't be so bad after all.

'Will you be at the gathering tomorrow?' one woman asked.

Another one said, 'We don't want to rush you into things. You've only just got here! But—'

'It would be wonderful if you could,' another said.

'Would you come, Toy?' Thorsgift asked, and Affie saw how the others turned and looked at him, because he addressed Odinstoy so familiarly. So she moved closer to Odinstoy herself.

'I'll be there,' Odinstoy said.

That went down well.

'Will you speak?' a woman asked. 'Would you – would you – speak for Him?'

'Give her a chance to catch herself up!' said another.

'Maybe I will speak,' Odinstoy said. 'If He comes to me, I'll speak for Him.'

There was a little gasp, a catching of breath.

But Affie had her share of admiration too. She was the new God-speaker's wife and sister, after all. People wanted to make themselves known to her, to make a favourable impression on her, and that was gratifying – though a little vexing when she saw them trying to do the same with Gift, the brat.

But she was told she was pretty, and her hair was admired. 'Is it something you put in it that makes it –' The woman flicked her hand in an attempt to express the way colours shimmered and flickered through the waves of Affie's hair.

'No.' Affie smiled and, glancing round, saw again that she was by far the most beautiful person in the tiny room. It wasn't vanity: it was a simple fact. 'It grows like that.'

They looked at her raptly; watched the colours changing to orange and pink.

'I was engineered,' Affie explained. 'Before I was born. My parents had me engineered. I think it's jellyfish genes that make my hair do that.'

They stared more. 'Oh. I've heard something about that,' one said, at last.

It was afternoon before the party broke up, and then Affie, Odinstoy and Gift left with them, because a couple of the women had offered to show them around the village.

'You'll soon feel at home,' one of the Ingas said. 'It isn't very big.'

'And everyone's friendly,' said a Thora.

It was strange, feeling that you were in a street, just as you might be on Earth, and then looking up and seeing the dome above you, with its honeycomb of rainbow bubbles, and its crane-tracks and maintenance pathways. Moments later, you would forget that you were in a dome, because there was a village green, with a duck-pond, and a place to play bowls, and tall trees. Only when you looked up to see the tops of the trees, did you see the roof of the dome again, and the violet sky beyond it.

They strolled around the pond, and Affie kept expecting to come up against the wall of the dome, but there was no feeling of being trapped inside a bubble. Three-quarter-domes and half-domes had been added to the central one, to extend the village, and it seemed to go on and on . . .

'That's the village hall,' Thora said, pointing out a thatched, half-timbered building. 'We have all sorts there.'

'Canton meetings, dances, fund-raisers – you'll get mails about them,' Inga said. 'You won't miss anything!'

'Will you be standing for the canton?' Thora asked.

'The –? What's a canton?' Affie said.

'Oh – hasn't anyone explained all that? I thought they would have done – you could have read up on it on the journey.'

There had been stuff, Affie remembered, that she'd been told to read – but it had all been boring stuff about councils and committees, and she'd kept putting it off and, in the end, hadn't bothered.

'Osbourne is a canton,' Inga continued. 'That's a – what's a canton, Thora?'

'It's an area,' Thora said firmly. 'A self-governing area. Osbourne is one. Ares is divided into several cantons. Then there's Olympus and . . . But I don't want to bore you. You'll learn it all as you go along.'

'It's like – politics?' Affie said.

'Exactly, yes,' Thora said. 'We really need honest, responsible people on the canton. It's quite usual for a God-speaker to be on it – in a year or two, you might want to stand.'

'Are you paid for it?' Affie asked. She'd never taken much notice of politics but she seemed to remember that, back on Earth, politicians had always seemed quite wealthy.

Inga and Thora both laughed. 'Well!' Thora said. 'In Ares, yes, but then, you see, Ares is Church of Mars, almost solidly Church of Mars.'

Odinstoy looked completely blank, and Affie looked puzzled.

'So they all worship Zeus and Apollo and Demeter—'

'Hermes and Diana and all those old, establishment Gods,' Inga said.

'Yes, like on Earth,' Thora explained. 'So they get money from Earth to support their churches—'

'And all sorts of subsidies and grants,' Inga said. 'It's a scandal.'

'It's the price we pay for being free-thinkers,' Thora said. 'What I'm trying to explain is that it's only Ares that's big enough to be able to pay their councillors; and you only get elected in the Ares cantons if you're Church of Mars. Anything else, and you don't stand a chance. That's why Osbourne – oh, and Haven, and Lewis, and some other independent cantons – that's why they got started. Free-thinkers started them, because they couldn't worship as they liked in Ares without being harassed; and they couldn't get good jobs. So gatherings clubbed together and raised money, and they started their own cantons, where they could live as they liked. Osbourne is one of the oldest, and Lewis is like us as well – they worship the Aesir, I mean.'

'Aesir?' Affie said, feeling as if she was in a fog.

Thora looked at her curiously. 'Odin, dear, and Thor, Frey, Freya – our Gods.'

'Oh,' Affie said.

'They're called the Aesir,' Thora said.

'Haven is Presleyan,' Inga said. 'They worship Elvis Presley.'

'What I was trying to say,' Thora continued, 'is that to be a councillor in places like Osbourne, you have to have your own income, or do two jobs – councillor and something else. It's hard work. That's why we need good people. Think about it.' She pointed at a pretty little house, with tubs of flowers outside. 'The Bentons live there – you can buy bread from them. Very good bread too.'

'That's the village shop – it's a co-op. All local produce – we all buy from there.'

'You can always get a taxi from the square.'

'We haven't got a doctor here, but you can speak to one on-line – the hospital's in the city.'

'You'll probably have to go to the city to buy a bonder as well,' Inga said, 'though there might be one for sale around here. Do you want me to ask around?'

There was a silence. Thora rolled an eye at Inga, in a way that told Affie she had heard about Odinstoy's strange attitude to bonders. Affie held her breath, in the hope that Odinstoy might have seen sense.

'I shall never own a bonder,' Odinstoy said.

'Everybody's so excited about meeting you!' Thora said, in a rush to change the subject. 'We can't wait to hear you speak!'

Odin Speaks

'You should see the Temple of Odin where I come from, on Earth,' Affie said. 'It's big – oh, three times as big as this place. And it's dark – lit by long fires, so it all –' She waggled her fingers to try and describe the way the fire-light glimmered through the dimness. Her audience of young girls and their mothers listened raptly, while gazing at her lovely face and her hair, which was full of shifting cloud-patterns in orange and pink. 'There are tree-trunks holding up the roof and statues and – well, it's, like, *hugely* special.'

'We've got nowhere like that,' one of the girls said. They were standing in Osbourne's town hall which, despite its thatched exterior, was a simple box inside, with smooth, pale-green walls. At one end was a small stage, with a screen, speakers and lights. It was a place for town meet-ings about stray dogs and the litter problem, not a temple for worship.

'Odin and Thor haven't been worshipped on Mars for very long,' said a woman. 'You'll find temples to Zeus – they've got the money – but not to our Odin.'

'We've got Odinstoy now, though,' said another of the girls. 'She's wonderful, isn't she?'

Yes, she is wonderful, Affie thought. You've no idea how wonderful. And she's *my* friend.

She and Odinstoy had dressed carefully that morning, in clothes they'd been given by their neighbours 'until you can get to the shops'. Odinstoy had chosen a white-and-blue striped shirt – blue was Odin's colour – and a pair of faded blue trousers. It would be hard to tell, at first glance, whether she was a boy or a woman.

Affie had chosen a dress which had once belonged to one of Rebecca's daughters. She didn't much like wearing cast-offs, but this one was of excellent quality and hardly worn. 'She bought it and then decided she didn't like it,' Rebecca said. 'Never wore it.' The dress had long sleeves, a wide scooped neck, a fitted bodice and a full swinging skirt, reaching to her knee. Coincidentally, it was also in Odin's colour: a pale but intense blue. That was lucky: but Affie wore it because it flattered her as well as any dress she could have chosen for herself.

They'd walked, with Gift between them, through the village until they reached the town hall. Many others had been going the same way; most of the people of Osbourne followed the Aesir faith. And there had been taxis drawing up in the square, bringing people from other settlements, and even from Ares.

Affie saw the way people looked at them and whispered and drew the attention of others to them. It was gratifying. She drew herself up, raised her head, dropped her shoulders, sucked in her stomach, and smiled as she looked about her. Her hair, she knew, would be shimmering with pink and magenta lights. She saw the quick turn of male heads as they tried not to be caught looking at her. Here and there she caught the quick lift of eyebrows that meant a man had been surprised and pleased by the sight of her. Very gratifying – except that they thought she was Odinstoy's wife. That might give them a thrill, but wasn't going to help her find a rich husband. Oh well. Early days.

A girl – she would be called Inga or Thora, for sure – came bouncing up to them, beaming. 'Leander Fitzpatrick's here! With a camera!'

Odinstoy smiled. Affie said, 'That's nice.'

The girl was impatient. 'They say it means you're going to speak, Odinstoy. Are you?'

Other girls had joined her. They walked with them, some of them walking backwards, waiting for an answer.

Odinstoy said, 'If Odin wishes me to speak . . .'

Affie felt like giggling. Of course Odinstoy was going to speak. Affie had, herself, mailed Leander to let him know that she was. After all, these people had paid their passage from Earth, had put them up in the hotel, and provided the cramped little hut they lived in and the clothes they wore. They would expect something in return, and the sooner the better.

Odinstoy suddenly reached out to one of the girls, and cupped her hand about her head. She stopped, and the girl did too. They stared at each other, Odinstoy intent, the girl rather frightened. The other girls and Affie halted, and they also stared. Even Affie didn't know what was going on. No one quite dared to giggle.

Odinstoy said, 'You are hurt, but she is in Odin's hand now.'

The girl's face became truly scared. Everyone else was enthralled.

'All things pass,' Odinstoy said, 'however much they hurt. This will pass too.'

The girl said, 'How—?' and her voice broke into tears.

Another girl said, 'How did you know?' To everyone else, she explained, 'Bergara's grandmother died. Three days ago.'

There was a gasp, and everyone's stare returned to Odinstoy, who said: 'She is in Odin's hand. Set a place for her at Yule.' She took her hand from the girl's head and went on. The girls scattered, each running off to tell friends and family.

'How *did* you know?' Affie had asked, quietly.

'Odin told me.'

Affie took a sudden, sharp look at her, as if meaning to catch her out. Odinstoy wasn't even looking at her, but watching Gift, who was wandering among the people a few metres away. My Gods, Affie thought, and felt a shiver: Odin really, really does talk with her. How else could she know? If Odinstoy had known by normal means about this girl's grandmother's death, then Affie would have known too. It was strange how respect for someone ebbed when you lived closely with them, no matter how strange they really were. And Affie wasn't exactly pleased to be reminded of Odinstoy's gifts. It meant that she always had to accept that Odinstoy was right, even when she said things Affie didn't like, such as, 'It's wrong to keep a bonder'. It made life difficult.

They'd gone into the town hall. Inside, long tables were set with drinks and plates of raven-buns. People were gathered around these tables, chattering, weaving to and fro, finding friends. Odinstoy and Affie came to a halt in the centre of the hall, and a space cleared around them.

Through the crowd came Leander Fitzpatrick. To Affie he held out both hands and said, 'Sweetheart! You're just as lovely as I remember! We must meet up . . . Odinstoy! Could you come and talk to camera, darling? Just a few words.'

Odinstoy smiled and followed him, the people pressing aside to let them pass. The cameraman was waiting with his camera on his shoulder. 'If you could stand against the wall . . .' he said.

'If you would, please, Odinstoy; this won't take long,' said Leander.

Odinstoy obligingly stood against the pale-green wall, and the cameraman aimed his lens at her. People watched, but kept well back.

'Could you tell us how you feel,' Leander said, 'as you attend your first – er – gathering on Mars?'

Odinstoy stared into the camera as they all waited for her reply. Then her attention wandered. She walked away from the spot where she'd been placed. Leander looked surprised, but the cameraman kept filming, recording the surprise on the faces of people as Odinstoy came among them.

She reached for someone and drew – no, pulled – forward someone who was reluctant to come – a bonder who'd been standing at the back of the crowd, against the wall. Odinstoy embraced her and kissed her cheek, in front of everyone.

Oh, why are you *doing* this? Affie thought. We all know you were a bonder; there's no need to keep reminding us. Besides – she looked around at the people near her – it won't play well. Some faces were fascinated, but many others were puzzled or disapproving.

To the bonder, Odinstoy said, 'The baby will be a girl. And happy. There will be love for her. And you.'

The expressions on the face of the bonder-girl were quick and shifting: bewilderment and fear; then sheer astonishment, changing to radiant delight. Odinstoy kissed her again, and then turned back to the camera. 'Odin wants me to be here,' she said, and walked away to join those around the table and help herself to a bun.

Leander Fitzpatrick looked shocked for a second, but then said to his cameraman, 'No, we'll go with that, go with that.'

'Course we bloody will,' said the cameraman.

Affie looked round and saw faces in the crowd that were angered. She plunged after Odinstoy. When she reached her, she'd stopped to talk to Rebecca and Heimdal, who were introducing her to another tall Martian man, dressed all in black.

Heimdal was saying, 'I see the Church of Mars is with us.'

The black-clothed man, Rebecca and Odinstoy all looked in the same direction – at someone on the other side of the room. Affie looked too, but she didn't know which person in particular they were looking at.

'They were bound to send someone,' said the black-clothed man. 'My old friends – keeping an eye on me!'

'Oh, Affie,' Rebecca said, 'this is Freyslove. He leads our gathering.'

'My given name was Julius,' said the man in black, stooping down to speak to her. He had an earnest manner. 'I took the name Freyslove when I came to the Aesir – about five years ago.'

'And you're a speaker already!' Affie said.

Freyslove looked both pleased and embarrassed. 'I wanted to give something back to the community that had taken me in,' he said, 'so I volunteered to lead the gatherings, and—'

'Oh, Freyslove isn't a *God-speaker*,' Rebecca said.

'No,' Freyslove agreed, giving Rebecca a slightly annoyed glance. 'People seem to like it when I lead the gatherings –'

'Oh yes, you do a wonderful job,' Rebecca murmured.

'– but I can't claim that Odin speaks directly into my ear! Alas! But it's such an honour to welcome a real God-speaker like Odinstoy – and you, Affie.'

76

Somehow, Affie doubted it. She glanced at Odinstoy, to see what she thought, but Odinstoy's face held no expression but an empty, friendly smile.

'You'll say a few words to the gathering?' Freyslove said. 'I'll introduce you—'

Thorsgift came up, put an arm around Odinstoy and, stooping, kissed her cheek. 'I've been looking for you. You're going to speak for Odin?'

Freyslove, his words broken off, stared for an eye's-blink, then said, 'I'd prepared a sermon, but of course, if Odinstoy wishes—'

'Yes! Odinstoy!' Thorsgift said, and his words were echoed by people who had added themselves to the edges of their group.

'Go on, Odinstoy!'

'Go on!'

'I'll speak,' she said, 'if Odin wishes it.' She looked round. 'Where's Gift?'

Lost for good, let's hope, Affie thought; but she made a show of looking for him, pushing through the crowd. She came near the tables, where some people were helping themselves to more beer or wine. Standing still, looking round, she heard a man near her say, 'When has Odin ever been a God of bonders?'

Affie turned towards the voice and saw a heavily-built, elderly man – quite plainly elderly, he'd done nothing to hide it. His companion, a woman equally elderly, grey-haired, wrinkles and all, nudged him and nodded towards Affie. The man glanced towards her, and said, just as loudly,

'Well, Odin was always a God of kings and the like.' Obviously, he considered himself 'the like'. 'If our bonders all start fancying themselves God-speakers, where shall we be?'

Affie moved away, thinking that Odinstoy should be more careful. For every person she thrilled with her embracing of bonders, she annoyed another.

She didn't have a chance to say anything like that when she found Odinstoy again. There were too many people round her, too much chatter, and Odinstoy was too busy pulling faces with Gift, who'd been restored to her. The brat.

Then a bell rang, and the noise of chatter lessened, and everyone moved towards the stage at the further end of the hall. Rebecca and Heimdal made their way to the front, ushering Affie and Odinstoy with them, Heimdal even carrying Gift. There were no seats. People shuffled into their place in the crowd, hushed children, looked up, and a quiet fell.

Freyslove was standing on the stage, in his high-necked black sweater and his neat beard. 'Welcome to you all!' he called out. 'You are all welcome.' He looked down at Affie and Odinstoy. 'And welcome especially to two new members of our gathering –' There was appreciative laughter and a shifting in the crowd as people realised who he meant. '– Odinstoy, and her wife, Freya. Odinstoy, our new God-speaker!' There was applause, and Freyslove joined in.

Someone – it was a woman's voice, a young voice – called out, 'Will Odinstoy speak for us?'

Other voices whooped, called out, 'Yes!' Freyslove looked down at Odinstoy again. Affie looked at her too, willing her to agree, but Odinstoy shook her head. Freyslove said, 'I think . . . Will she? No – I don't think – No? It looks like you're stuck with me.' A mock groan went up. 'So sorry. Shall we sing?'

The words of the hymn appeared on a screen behind and above Freyslove's head, and music played from speakers. The gathering obediently raised its voice in song:

> *'Mother,*
> *Mother,*
> *Mother!*
> *Hail to you, Mother of us all!*
> *Come to Odin, come to him!*
> *Come, Odin's Queen!*
> *Embrace,*
> *Embrace,*
> *Embrace your Lord . . .'*

After the hymn, Freyslove spoke again. 'I've been thinking a lot about bridges lately. I want to speak to you today about bridges. If you think about it,' he urged them kindly, 'the Space-El that brought Odinstoy to us is a *kind* of bridge. A bridge takes us from here –' he marked a place in the air with his hand '– to here.' He marked another place, about a metre away. 'You're *here*.' He indicated the first place again. 'And you want to be *here*.' He indicated the second place. 'So what do you do?'

His manner suggested that if they tried very, very hard, they might figure it out.

I don't know, Affie thought. Take a taxi? Who is this idiot?

'You use a *bridge*,' Freyslove told them. 'You cross to the other side using a bridge. A bridge brings people together. And, you know, sometimes *we* can be bridges.'

Affie looked at the faces of the people near her, but they were all listening politely.

'When people are in different places, when they're not reaching out to each other, then *we*, each one of us, can be a bridge . . .'

Odinstoy, standing beside Affie, looking up at Freyslove, felt Odin lean close at her right shoulder. She felt the loom and weight of Him; she almost smelt Him – a muskiness. She heard His voice and His order. *Now!*

Affie, still listening with irritation to Freyslove, felt a movement at her side and looked round. Odinstoy was stepping up onto the stage. She almost reached out to stop her.

Odinstoy stood on the stage, a little distance from Freyslove, and faced the audience. The attention of many, many people locked on her at once. She felt a jolt of pure fear: a small creature with many attentive eyes on it.

Then, again, the loom at her shoulder, the voice in her right ear: *Take them from him*. She calmed. Odin was with her.

Freyslove, facing slightly away from her, talking to the gathering, hadn't noticed she was there. He was still talking about bridges; about how each one of them could be a bridge, a rainbow bridge, to bring people to Thor, to Frey, to Odin . . . He noticed that the attention of the people was no longer with him. The gaps between his words lengthened as he looked here and there, trying to puzzle out why – and then he followed the direction of their eyes and saw Odinstoy. 'Oh—' he said, and stopped.

The gathering became quiet, and the silence intensified as Odinstoy neither moved nor spoke. A child's voice, suddenly piping up, was sharply hushed.

Affie, watching from the front row, was elated. Odinstoy was doing what she'd wanted her to do. Come on, she urged, in her head. Come on, girl. Make our future.

Odinstoy slowly raised her lowered head until she was looking out over the audience. They expected her to speak, but she kept silent. She must keep silent, she knew, until it seemed everyone was close to screaming with impatience. And then she must keep silent for longer still.

Affie felt about to throw a fit. Odinstoy just stood there, not moving, not speaking – wasting their chance. She was boring the people.

Slowly, Odinstoy tipped back her head until they could see only her throat. A child yipped, and someone giggled, and Affie looked round, scared. It was all going to go wrong now. People would laugh. Walk out.

At the child's noise, Odinstoy almost flinched and had to stretch her fingers to keep them from clenching into fists. Not yet . . . Not yet . . . Make them wait. Slowly, slowly, she lowered her head. Again, she stared out over the audience in silence. And they waited. They didn't jeer or heckle; they didn't leave. They waited. They held their breaths and waited.

Odinstoy spoke. From the small figure on the stage came the voice of a man: deep, clipped, barking out the words with flat, dismissive authority. He – She – Odinstoy or Odin – said, 'Look you for wisdom? Find one who has travelled far.'

The audience gave a great collective gasp of astonishment and recognition. Excepting the small children, everyone there recognised a close echo of a verse from The Words of The High One, the words of Odin Himself.

And then there rose another exclamation, and people all over the hall turned to one another, as the significance of the words came to them. Two people stood on the stage. Which of them had travelled further?

'One who has travelled,' said the man's voice from the girl's body, 'can judge rightly those they meet. One who has travelled knows the ways of the worlds.'

Freyslove stepped down into the audience. He didn't, Affie thought, look the happiest man she'd ever seen. Another sound rose from the crowd, one that made Affie turn. It didn't come from the whole crowd, but it was an angry sound, a protesting growl.

Angry, Affie thought: they're angry. Toy had better come down, quick. She looked up at her, willing her to sense the mood of the crowd and come down from the stage.

But Odinstoy *had* sensed the mood of the crowd, and

had measured it far more accurately than Affie. Some were angry. Good. Far more were intrigued, excited, and keen to hear more. She didn't leave the stage, but did what Odin prompted her to do. Slowly, she raised her right arm until it was pointed straight up, the forefinger extended. She held that pose, held it and held it and held it, until her arm ached.

The growling in the crowd fell away. There was whispering, and then silence.

The uplifted, pointing arm was connecting in people's heads with an uplifted spear. Odin's spear, his symbol. Odin's spear, upheld by a woman – Valkyrie, the warrior-women, Odin's messengers and servants.

Some in the crowd felt their scalps tingle, then felt chills, felt their breath come short as Odin came amongst them. They felt the loom of His bulk behind them, and some started and half turned as the hair stirred on the backs of their necks.

Odinstoy – or Odin – said, 'Our native land is dear to us all – if we can enjoy what is ours with peace and plenty!'

Again, that echo of words they all knew, but seeming more direct than they ever had before, coming straight from the mouth of Odin.

'Your ancestors made this land for you,' Odin said, and everyone there thought of their ancestor trees in their computers.

'Their blood is mixed with the regolith,' Odin said. 'That's why it's red. Treasure the land they made for you.'

Her upraised arm dropped to her side. She staggered, and sat down at the edge of the stage. The audience said, 'Oooh,' and the people at the front rushed forward to help.

Affie, pushing her way through the knot of people, found Odinstoy shaking her head and saying, 'I'm all right . . . I'm fine . . . Where's Gift?'

'He's here.' Rebecca had him, and had elbowed her way to Odinstoy's side.

'Can I . . . be somewhere quiet? Can I have a drink?'

'Will you move back, please?' Rebecca said loudly to the people around them. 'Will you let us through?' She led them to an office behind the stage, just Odinstoy, Affie, Gift and Rebecca; and Rebecca left them to find Odinstoy a drink.

Odinstoy stopped drooping in her chair, sat up and grinned.

'You should be more careful,' Affie said. 'You've made people angry.'

Odinstoy said, 'Good.'

Memo

Zeuslove was watching television.

The screen showed the interior of a drab town hall. A group of women and girls grinned at the camera.

'What did you make of Odinstoy?' asked the off-screen voice of the ubiquitous Leander Fitzpatrick.

'Oh, very good,' said the woman. 'Very good indeed.'

'Wonderful!' said the girls in chorus, pulling ecstatic faces. 'Fantastic! Fabulous!'

The picture cut to an older woman with a serious expression, who said, 'I felt *Him* among us – didn't you? That's what I come to gathering for. *He* was here.'

The picture changed. A heavy-set man said, 'Outrageous. A complete performance. A sham. All she did was recite The Words of Odin. *I* can do that.'

The man beside him said, 'She's a bonder—'

'Was,' came Leander's voice.

'Let me finish, young man. Was a bonder, is a bonder, what's the difference? A bonder can't speak for Odin. It's nonsense. She's a charlatan, nothing more.'

The serious woman appeared again. 'Of *course* she

speaks for Odin. I've never heard Odin speak more clearly. She was wonderful. Inspiring.'

Zeuslove switched from the broadcast to the memo he'd been mailed, with an account of Odinstoy's speaking. There were clips attached, filmed on his informant's phone: the quality wasn't great, but they were good enough for Zeuslove to form an idea of Odinstoy's ability.

His reporter, in the memo, warned him not to be lulled by those members of the gathering who expressed outrage and appeared to reject Odinstoy. 'They were only a few. The girl has an appeal.'

Zeuslove agreed. It was a foolish man who under-estimated his enemy. The girl indeed had appeal – for all the wrong reasons. There was the appeal to the sex-instinct: always dangerous in the way it overruled reason. The young and inexperienced were always at risk of being overwhelmed by it. Odinstoy's boyish appear-ance in her boy's clothes was a deliberate ploy to widen her appeal.

And the very fact that she annoyed the more tradi-tional of the Aesir Faith as much as she annoyed Zeuslove was calculated to increase her appeal to that childish and self-aggrandising section of the population that liked to fancy itself 'individualistic' and 'rebellious' – as if there was something original or praiseworthy about selfishness.

But he had to keep a sense of proportion. Panicking, and investing the threat that was Odinstoy with far more power than in fact it had, would help no one but Odinstoy.

MEMO

The little minds that were swayed by her could be as easily swayed back again, given the right tools. And, in order to find those tools, he needed to know more.

'Command. Create memo . . .'

Listening to Odin

Odin spoke to Odinstoy, but He was standing at a distance, speaking quietly. She could hear His voice, knew He was telling her something important, but couldn't distinguish His words.

Not that He spoke in words – or not solely in words. There would be a feeling of something drawing near her, of hanging over her; and often there was a mood with it, so she could say: something bad, or: something good. She would pay attention, attend to the feeling and ask it: What?

Sometimes she had to ask several times, making her mind blank and receptive; sometimes the answer came at once. The initial feeling of 'something good' or 'something bad' would become clearer. There would be frail images, like memories of dreams; and sometimes a verse or a few lines from the rune poems or The Words of The High One would rise into her mind. The words were often enough to express what Odin told her, even if obliquely.

But they weren't enough now. Odin was trying to tell her something that felt much bigger than anything He had told her before. It loomed in her mind, so large that it was almost smothering.

It never went away. If she was with others and their chatter, if she was playing with Gift, if she was cooking or trying to sleep, always she could feel that great Something hovering at the edges of her mind, trying to push in.

She tried to let it in. Lying in bed, staring at the dark ceiling, she asked: What? What is it?

The verses about 'Native Land' whispered in her head, but quickly died. They weren't right; it wasn't that. The words about Freyja, the Goddess, came to her briefly, but Odin said: *No. No.*

Tell me, she said. What is it? Good? Bad? Shouldn't we have come here? Is it something we should do now we're here? What?

She needed to find quiet, to be able to listen hard, to let the answer slowly form in her mind and rise to the surface, but she had no time. Everyone in Osbourne knew her now, and almost everyone wanted to speak to her. If she took Gift to look at the ducks, they were stopped constantly. Women wanted to introduce their children to her, wanted her to kiss their baby, or to ask her advice on something, which might be anything from legal matters to how to prevent their cakes from sinking, or the best way of disciplining their bonder. ('Don't,' Odinstoy said.)

'You are wonderful,' they said. 'You have such a gift. It must be quite frightening. You must be so proud.'

It was a puzzling view. Odinstoy considered it no more a gift than walking or sneezing. Speaking for Odin was simply something she could do, and until Odin took the ability away, she intended to make the best of it. It was no more something to be proud of than the ability to yawn, and no more frightening than being alive. She knew Odin could take away the knack at any moment – but so He would with life.

When the women weren't chattering at her – or bringing her gifts of food to her door – then there was Thorsgift. He was always turning up. Would she and Gift like to take a walk? His mother had just made some cakes, and they were all invited round to try them. Or, there was a dance over in Jesmond; would she like to go? Affie could come too, if she liked. (If she had to, he meant.)

Thorsgift fancied he loved her, Odinstoy knew that. She also knew that, if she hadn't been a God-speaker, he wouldn't have looked at her. The idea that he would have loved her if she'd still been a bonder when they'd met was laughable. He wouldn't have seen or heard her. She would have been less visible to him than the furniture. Odinstoy therefore felt entitled to use Thorsgift when he was useful, without feeling anything for him except a slight contempt. 'If there is one you trust not, but good you would have of him,' said Odin, 'then speak him fair, and pay him measure for measure.'

It was hard to get rid of Thorsgift while speaking him fair; but all the time she talked with him, she could hear Odin trying to talk to her.

Men came calling too, saying they had a spare day and

were there any jobs she needed doing? Even children came calling. They would giggle and run away.

'They just want to look at The Voice of Odin,' Affie said.

Affie's voice was a constant noise.

'That Thorsgift. He's always hovering about, with his tongue drooling. He just wants to be seen with you, he thinks it makes him so special. Well, *I'm* your wife.'

Affie saying, 'You should give consultations. Hire a hall. Make money somehow.'

Affie saying, 'We're on Mars now; we've got to get on with our lives. This God-speaking's all very well, but you need to make some money.'

Affie saying, 'We are going to go to that party, aren't we? We are, aren't we?'

She was as bothersome as flies about your head.

'We *are* going, aren't we?'

'Go yourself,' Odinstoy said.

'But we're both invited! You must come!'

'I don't want to come.'

'Leander will expect you to come! We're supposed to be *married*.'

'Go yourself!'

Affie was quiet then, because when Odinstoy lost her temper, she was frightening.

Gift brought a toy, a woolly sheep, to Odinstoy, who took it, but simply held it limply. 'Play!' Gift said, pulling at her arm. 'Play!'

To his surprise – to Affie's amazement – Odinstoy

pushed him away. Gift drew back towards Affie and looked at her, as if asking if she knew what he'd done wrong.

'What's the story?' Affie asked.

'Go to your party. And leave me alone.'

'The invitation's for us both, not—'

'Leave me alone!'

Affie and Gift looked at each other. Affie said, 'Shall we go and look at the ducks?' Looking at ducks, especially in Gift's company, was not something Affie would normally have chosen to do, but it was better for everybody if Odinstoy was kept in a good temper.

He grinned at her, so she stood up and offered him her hand. She hoped the ducks knew how much they were being honoured.

They were by the door, hand in hand, when Odinstoy said, 'Look after him for me.'

Affie glanced round, puzzled. She *was* looking after the brat, so why ask?

'I won't be here when you get back. Look after him.'

Affie felt fright flutter under her breastbone. She looked at Gift, but he was trying to reach the door handle and chattering about ducks. 'Where are you going?' Where could she go? Where did they know on Mars?

'I don't know,' Odinstoy said.

'Well – when are you coming back?'

'I don't know.'

'But – how long are you going to leave me with him? Will you be back before the party?'

Odinstoy leaped to her feet, throwing her arms into the air. 'I don't know!'

Affie opened the door and bundled Gift through it.

The party was that night and Affie was going to go. Odinstoy hadn't come back, but that wasn't going to stop her. She couldn't let it stop her. This party was important. She might meet a rich Martian who would fall in love with her. She might meet a rich Martian businessman who would give her the money to start a fashion design business – *and* fall in love with her . . .

It had been two days since she'd come back from the duck-pond with Gift to find that Odinstoy had gone. She refused – *refused* – to worry about Odinstoy. Odinstoy was an adult, and a tough bonder who could survive anything. She'd chosen to go off, so let her . . .

Besides, by the second day, they'd had an idea where she was. A man named Ketil Lulworth, who was a maintenance engineer, had let Odinstoy into the system of maintenance ladders and platforms that led up into the height of the dome. He'd had to let her up there, he'd said, because she'd wanted to get as high above the world as she could, to talk to the God, just like the old priestesses of ancient times.

So *stay* up there, Affie thought, if that's what you want.

Only, no; because then she'd be stuck with Gift.

And she had to go to that party. She'd worked out what she was going to wear – making the best of a bad job – and she'd worked out how she was going to get there.

Now she had to work out what she was going to do with Gift.

Looking after him had been a constant pain. He was always wanting something to eat, which she then had to find and give to him, and whatever she gave him – a piece of bread, an apple – he didn't want. 'Leave it then,' Affie said, and he would scream like a brat. Or he'd want a drink. If she succeeded in finding something that he'd eat, he then wanted a drink. And then he wanted her to play with him, or tell him a story.

'Oh, play by yourself.' And he'd cry again. She didn't bother to wash him or change his clothes – well, he always made a huge fuss even when Odinstoy did it, so why make trouble for herself? When he fell asleep on the floor, she left him there – why struggle to make him go to bed? She did throw the rug over him.

She certainly wasn't taking him to the party. And she certainly wasn't going to miss it, either.

When Odinstoy still hadn't come back by noon, Affie said to Gift, 'You've got to have a shower.'

'No!'

Affie didn't waste time trying to persuade him, but hauled him into the shower room. He twisted and struggled, he howled and kicked her. She hit him. She got them both, fully-clothed, into the sonic, because it was easier. Gift was still screaming, lost in rage, fighting to get out. She held the door shut and pressed the buttons. A minute later she staggered out, and Gift fell out, red-faced and sobbing with temper.

'Hate you!' He punched her leg.

She held his hands and shook him. 'Not half as much as I hate you!' At least there was no need to change his clothes now; that saved time and trouble. 'Let's go and see Rebecca,' she shouted above his screams. 'You like Rebecca.'

'No no no no!'

She seized him by both wrists and hoisted him off the floor. 'You – are – *going* – to – Rebecca!'

'No no no – hate Affie!'

She managed to get him out of the house, but then he used all his weight and succeeded in lying on the ground, where he kicked and screamed.

'Lie there, then,' Affie said, and walked off. She really didn't care if he lay there and screamed until he choked. Of course, he got up and ran after her.

She walked along the streets of small dwellings towards Rebecca's place. High above was the roof of the dome with its hexagons, faintly crossed by bridges. If Odinstoy was still up there, could she hear Gift bawling? If she could, perhaps she'd come down.

'Oh Affie – whatever is the matter with Gift?'

Inga Mendip had crossed from the other side of the street. Why couldn't she do the polite thing and ignore them?

'Where's Odinstoy? Has she not come back yet?'

Would I be lumbered with the brat if she had? Affie thought. Aloud she said, 'I'm just taking him to Rebecca . . .'

95

Inga had stooped over Gift to try and calm him, but Gift, presented with a fresh audience, threw himself on the ground and screamed again – not quite as loudly as before, though. He was tiring.

'He won't behave for me,' Affie said, raising her voice to be heard. 'And I have . . . an appointment –' that sounded important and official '– an appointment in Ares. I can't take him – especially not like this.'

'I'll have him,' Inga said promptly.

Was the woman mad?

'No trouble at all,' Inga said.

The woman *was* mad. 'Thank you,' Affie said. 'Er – can I leave him with you now? I have to get ready.'

'You leave Gift to me. Don't worry about him at all.'

I won't, Affie thought, as she ran back towards her own house with a smile and a wave. Gift, who didn't want to be with her, raised a fresh scream of rage as he saw her leaving. There was no pleasing the brat.

Affie didn't know what Odinstoy would think of her child being handed over to the first person she met in the street. Not much, probably. But then, she shouldn't go off and dump him on Affie . . .

The view was distorted by the thick, hexagonal bubbles in each frame of the dome's skeleton, throwing rainbow lights across the vision; but it was a view of rich green, lush Martian fields, mile after mile of them, under a violet sky. There was corn, the maintenance men had said, growing far higher than even a Martian man. There was wheat, and potatoes, carrots, swedes . . . Martian soil was fertile. In miniature domes – or rather under long, arched tunnels that ran for miles, reflecting light – grew tomatoes, lettuces, strawberries; 'Oh, all sorts of fruit,' the maintenance men said.

'It's all been engineered,' said one. 'It's warmer on Earth, isn't it?'

'But it grows!' said another. 'Plant a bread roll, you get a tree full of hot-buttered-roll fruit!'

Odinstoy climbed higher into the dome. The ladders climbed from platform to platform right into the highest curve of the dome. One of the maintenance men had stamped on a narrow bridge, making it shiver. 'Spider's silk! Nothing stronger!' The maintenance network had something of the fragility of a spider's web. 'It has to give and flex with the dome – it might feel shaky but it's stronger that way.'

Look over the rails and you looked down into the dome, at roads and the roofs of houses, at the tops of trees. She was still under a roof, but high up there on the slightly swaying platform, she felt far away from people and houses and gatherings and everyday life. Even Gift seemed far away, though a sense of him, as always, pulsed under her breastbone, at her centre. The height and isolation were what she needed. The priestesses of Odin in ancient times, the völvas, had mounted up onto high platforms to speak to the God.

She roamed about the bridges and platforms, descending, climbing, sometimes sitting in the corner of a platform for hours. She met maintenance crews – they knew who she was and let her be – but for most of the time she was alone. It was cold up there, in the height of the dome, and she was hungry, having a flask of water with her, but no food. That was as it should be. Get back to the starkest, simplest of states – a cold body, a hungry belly – and the voice of the God would come through.

Mars had forests. She could see them, distortedly, through the bubbles of the dome. They broke up the fields, forests of giant fern and horsetail, helping to fix earth and make oxygen.

There were rivers and lakes, but no sign from here of the gigantic mountains and canyons that Thorsgift had boasted of. But this was a man-made Mars, a Mars born of a union between nature and man, between nature and science . . . Odin leaned close and whispered in her ear.

'Affie! Dearling! You are gorgeousness made flesh. *So* glad you could come.' Leander stooped, and he and Affie air-kissed. As he straightened, he was looking behind her. 'No Odinstoy . . .?'

'Oh, she's meditating or something. Talking to Odin. Couldn't come.'

'Well, I'm so happy *you* came. Now . . . Who would like to meet the most beautiful girl on Mars?'

'Oh, you flatterer, I shan't listen to you!' Affie said, enjoying herself and knowing as she looked round that, if not the most beautiful girl on Mars, she was certainly the most beautiful in that room. (And was it likely that there was one more beautiful on Mars? No.)

It had been difficult deciding what to wear. The cast-off clothes given to her were of good material and well made, but not stylish and not suitable, in Affie's opinion, for a party. They were all far too dull – long, high-necked, long-sleeved. The blue dress was pretty, but too demure and, besides, she'd already worn it in public.

She'd finally decided on a pair of black trousers and, as a top, a little violet camisole. Her hair she simply let hang loose – it rippled with bright-pink and red patterns. She wore no make-up, either, since she had none.

She'd left the house and walked to the square for a taxi. Those people she passed stared. Even those who knew her didn't speak; just stared. I must be looking wonderful, Affie thought.

There was a taxi waiting. She climbed inside, keyed in her ID number and her destination, and away the taxi went.

The drive was long enough for her to feel anxious about the evening ahead of her, and when the taxi drew up outside the restaurant, and she saw all the people outside at tables, and thronging between shops and cinemas and theatres, she felt afraid. This didn't look like the Mars she'd seen until now, and these people seemed too lively, too attractive, too stylish, to be Martian.

But she'd come alone, in defiance of Odinstoy. She had to go in. Programming the taxi to return to Osbourne, she got out. The taxi slid away, leaving her.

She refused to look around her; refused to look too closely at the people who made up the crowds. They would intimidate her. Instead she raised her head while lowering her shoulders, sucked in her stomach, and sashayed into the restaurant.

There was a mirrored wall opposite the entrance, and in it Affie was able to see herself full-length, as she hadn't been able to see herself since leaving Earth. She saw a most beautiful, graceful, curvaceous young woman, elegantly dressed, but with slim bare arms and smooth bare shoulders and showing just a little cleavage. Her glossy hair fell in curls over her shoulders, and sparkled with bright-pink cloud-patterns. All her nerves vanished.

A waiter directed her to the room upstairs where the party was held. She ran up, and gave her name to the person at the door, who announced her: 'Freya Atkinson!'

And then Leander Fitzpatrick came and kissed her, and ushered her into the party with a warm, attentive hand at the small of her back.

The room was lovely. There were white pillars, with gilded carving of fruit and flowers; and long tables of buffet food with cornucopias of fruit; and huge flower arrangements. There were women with their hair piled high and wearing gowns of flimsy drapery with one shoulder, or both, left bare. They had gold in their hair, round their necks and arms, and dangling from their ears. Some of the men were stylish enough to wear classical robes too; but even those who weren't wore expensive suits and shirts. This, Affie thought, looking round, is where I should be, among people like these – I should be in Ares, not stuck out in Osbourne with the yokels.

'I should introduce you to *everyone*!' Leander decided.

'Yes, everyone! I want to meet everyone – and their single sons!'

Leander hugged her to him. 'Naughty, naughty! And you a married lady! Dearling, you're a girl after my own heart!'

It felt as if she was introduced to everyone. 'Can I be awful and butt in for a moment? I *need* you to meet this lovely creature – isn't she divine?'

The whole evening became a blur of names, faces, smiles, laughter, hands shaken, cheeks kissed . . .

'*Odinstoy*'s wife . . . Did you catch my piece about Odinstoy?'

'I did, but . . . Remind me.'

'The God-speaker for Odin – out in Osbourne?'

'Oh *no* – Odin?'

'I saw that – is Odinstoy here?'

'She couldn't come,' Affie said. 'She's meditating. Deeply. On the meaning of life.'

People laughed, and Affie felt enormously witty and clever.

'Beautiful *and* funny,' a man said, and she felt dizzy with delight at herself.

'Having dangled her before you and dazzled you,' Leander said, 'I'm going to *snatch* her away . . . Oh, *dearlings*, let me introduce Affie—'

She met such important people – people from television,

though of course it was only Martian television. Producers, directors, actors, actresses, presenters. Of course, just as on Earth, some of them were bonders – so many creative people, such as actors and painters and musicians were – but if they were well known enough, they were treated just like anyone else.

She met engineers, who built mono-rails and did sewers and stuff like that. And doctors and councillors and – just, all sorts. None of them seemed short of money, and many of the men were rather good-looking . . .

As was the one who sidled alongside her as she was listening and laughing as a television presenter – he was well known on Mars, apparently – told how disastrously wrong one of his interviews had gone, what with equipment malfunctions, and the interviewee arriving late, and the research having got mixed up . . . He was a bonder, but *so* funny—

'You're Affie, aren't you?' said someone beside her, leaning close.

She turned to look at whoever it was. He was so close that she had to draw back her head to see him properly.

It was a young man, smiling, and almost handsome. His forehead was a little too high, his cheeks a little too hamsterish; his eyes a little too small and squinty. His skin was too pale against the darkness of his hair, brows and the lashes of his small eyes, while his lips were too red. Looking at him, Affie felt a faint struggle within her as she tried to see him as handsome – as she would prefer any young man who spoke to her to be – but was defeated by his oddity.

His parents surely hadn't had him designed to look like that? But maybe that was their idea of handsome? It was only a little off. If his eyes had been a little larger, his cheeks a little leaner, his complexion just a little less pale . . .

'You were with Odinstoy, weren't you? I saw her – at Osbourne.'

Does he know I'm supposed to be married to her? Affie thought. Unwilling to talk about her relationship to Odinstoy at all, she said, 'Oh – did you enjoy the gathering?'

'I did,' he said, and continued to look at her hard from beneath his brows, conveying that it wasn't the gathering he enjoyed so much as her presence. 'Very much.'

Affie looked away, though she couldn't stop herself smiling. It was delightful to be appreciated; but he was a bit impertinent, with that odd face, to come on to her. If only his eyes weren't so much like pin-holes thickly edged with black lashes. The lashes were dense because the eyes were so small.

'Odinstoy was wonderful,' she said, and glanced at him, to see how he would respond.

'No one could fail to be impressed with Odinstoy. A very special talent. But I confess, I couldn't take my eyes off you.'

'Oh? Did I have something caught in my teeth?'

He looked her in the face and said – exactly as she

had always hoped someone would say – 'You are the most beautiful woman I've ever seen.'

She knew it – she'd been designed to be; but it was so warming to be told that at least one other person did, indeed, think the same. She gazed at him as the words reverberated in her head. Pity, but his eyes were still too small.

'My name's Jason.'

She couldn't think of anything to say; and then Leander swooped again, linking his arm through hers. 'Stop flirting, Affie – or stop flirting with *him*, anyway, and come and flirt with the Archpriest of Demeter—'

She waved her fingers at Jason as she was towed away; and he waved his back, and smiled – or smirked. It was annoying that his face was odd, but perhaps it could be fixed . . .

Odinstoy sat on the bench in their small house. Above, in the loft-bed, Gift was asleep. Odinstoy was tired, but kept awake by an anger, a suppressed, slow-burning, long anger.

She heard Affie's stumbling feet on the path and rose, apparently quite calmly, stepped across the room and opened the door.

'Oh! Hello!' Affie said, and laughed.

'Quiet. Gift is asleep.'

'Oh! Sorry!' Affie got herself through the door. Odinstoy closed it gently. 'Hey, you're back!'

'I'm back,' Odinstoy said. She grabbed Affie by the

throat and shoved her against the wall. The shove wasn't so hard, but the grip on her throat was choking and painful, with sharp ends of strong, thin fingers and nails digging into Affie's flesh. The suddenness, the calculated, passionless violence, was deeply frightening. Affie, instantly chilled and sobered, goggled at Odinstoy's calm face.

'Keep quiet,' Odinstoy said. 'I don't want Gift woken.'

Affie put up her hands to try and loosen the hand about her neck, but she was afraid to struggle much, in case she made Odinstoy angry. You could never tell what a bonder might do.

'You left Gift on his own.'

Affie tried to say no, but couldn't get the sound out; tried to shake her head, but couldn't.

'If you ever leave him again –' Odinstoy gently, quietly thumped Affie's head against the wall '– I'll kill you.' She let Affie go and returned to the bench.

Affie leaned on the wall, massaging her neck. She'd been giggly, happy, and ready to chatter about the party when she'd found Odinstoy at home, but that euphoria had been dispelled in an instant, to be replaced by a queasily-thumping heart. She was trembling slightly, and was uneasily balanced between tears and rage. 'I *didn't* leave Gift on his own.'

'You left him.'

'I left him with Inga! He was fine!'

'He was with Rebecca,' Odinstoy said. 'Inga couldn't handle him. I left him with *you*.'

'You knew I was going to the party!' Affie would have said more, but Odinstoy stood again, and Affie shrank along the wall towards the little washroom. If need be, she could dart in there and lock herself inside.

'I had to speak to Odin. I left Gift with you – not with Inga or Rebecca.'

'I'm sorry,' Affie said. They were difficult words, but seemed the wisest at the moment. 'Is Gift all right?'

'He is now.'

Affie slid closer to the washroom door. 'Did Odin speak to you?'

'He did.'

'What did He say?'

Odinstoy sat again, and leaned back. There was a long silence. During it, Affie found herself thinking: Do I really care what Odin says? Did I ever? Odinstoy had seemed wonderful on Earth, because Affie had been a bonder then, and desperate, and Odinstoy had shown her some kindness. Anything Odinstoy did – like worship Odin – had seemed special. But at the party she'd glimpsed what it might be like to be free and rich again

She almost said, 'I want a divorce,' but stopped herself. Why annoy Odinstoy again?

Raising her head, Odinstoy said, 'I'll rest for a couple of days . . . After that, I'll take Gift with me. I won't trust you with him again. And you can go to all the parties you like.'

At this promise of freedom, Affie immediately felt terrified. Was she being deserted? How could she cope on her own? Who would look after her? 'Where are you going?'

'Travelling.'

'But where?'

'To talk with Odin. And Mars.'

Wandering

Just as Odinstoy had promised, she and Gift were gone when Affie woke. At first she pretended they weren't. Odinstoy had taken Gift to feed the ducks, as she often did, that was all. Affie got up, stepped in and out of the sonic shower, dressed and went into the tiny kitchen, telling herself that it was peaceful without Gift's endless chatter. She was glad to have a little time to herself.

It was annoying to have to make her own breakfast, but she settled for some fruit grown in Mars's hothouses – a banana, an apple and some berries – with a glass of orange-juice.

When she'd finished eating, she rinsed her plate, glass and knife, while daydreaming about the next party she would go to, and Jason, and how she was going to be rich . . . Then she looked at the computer and checked their mails. Nothing from Jason, but there was one from Leander, thanking her for being a Goddess, and promising to be in touch again soon. She sent one back, with her love, saying that his party had been Elysium.

She played some games, and searched the net to see

what clothes were available on Mars. Nothing, as far as she could see that was *really* . . .

She was still alone, two hours after getting up, and admitted to herself that Odinstoy had gone wandering, as she'd said she would. Affie, alone, felt panic, slight as yet, but rising. All those hours, stretching ahead of her, to be spent alone in this little cell – it was hardly bigger than a cell. What would she do with herself? And what would she *do*? Food – where did she get food on Mars? What would she buy it with? She had never had to organise herself, or cope with ordinary things like buying groceries, neither when she'd been rich, nor as a bonder.

She was feeling hungry again and didn't want to cook. All that work, and she'd only make a mess of it – and would then have to clear up the mess. Why wouldn't Odinstoy let them have a bonder?

She stood, thinking that she would go and see Rebecca. Or Inga. Or anyone. They'd be sure to offer her something to eat and drink; and she might be able to find a way to ask them for help.

She hadn't reached the door when the computer beeped. Jason! she thought. Or Odinstoy, saying she was coming back. Eagerly, she turned back to the screen. The message it displayed said that the call was from Jason.

Oh – Jason! He'd said she was the most beautiful woman he'd ever seen. Dropping down on her bed – still unmade – she said, 'Command. Open message.'

The screen opened to show Jason's face. Affie had converted him, in her memory, to a beautiful, dark man, and was disappointed to be reminded how hamsterish his face was. He smiled and said, 'Can I speak to Affie please?'

'Oh – command! Cam on!'

Jason, on-screen, smiled again as he saw her image appear before him. His eyes became small, black-edged slits against his white skin. 'It's so good to see you again, Affie. I haven't been able to stop thinking about you all night.'

Giggles thrilled through Affie, though she tried to suppress them. She felt warmed, more warmed and happy than she had since – when? What other person in her life hadn't been able to stop thinking about her? Her mother had found it easy enough, when she'd gone off to California and left Affie behind. She'd hardly ever seen her father, and when he'd decided to shoot himself, he hadn't been thinking of her. But she'd always believed that there was someone, somewhere, who would truly love her.

'I've been thinking a lot about you, too,' she said, her voice shaking.

'Could I come and see you?' Jason said.

'I'd like that,' Affie said, 'I'd completely like that.' And then she added, 'I'm all on my own here. I've been on my own for ages.' Tears came to her eyes, surprising and embarrassing her. She hadn't meant to whine like that. It wasn't sophisticated; it wasn't cool. Jason would be put off.

So she was relieved and grateful when he smiled and said, 'On your own? You? Why would someone so lovely ever be on their own?'

'Oh – it's because Odinstoy's gone away.'

'She doesn't deserve you. Doesn't know how to cherish you. Where's she gone?'

'I don't know – travelling. Exploring. She said she'd gone to talk with Odin.'

He laughed, and Affie was a little annoyed that he could laugh at Odinstoy or Odin. 'Well . . . If she's so tight with Odin, would she mind if I came and kept you company?'

Affie laughed delightedly.

'I could bring a picnic with me,' he said. 'Essentials like . . . chocolate . . . wine . . . strawberries . . .'

'Oooh! I love strawberries!'

'See you soon!' Jason said; and his image vanished from the screen. Affie felt a pang – but was comforted by the knowledge that he would soon be in the room with her.

Gift was happy. He sang a complicated, wordless song, rising up to high notes and swooping down to low ones, which made him chuckle. His mother laughed too, her eyes shining, sharing his joke and admiring him, egging him on, which made him even happier. He couldn't remember a happier time.

They were wandering, hand in hand and singing, through a place of many, many thick tangled stems. His mother said it was a vineyard, but he wasn't sure what that was. He could see it was inside a dome, like everywhere else – overhead were the six-sided bubbles of the roof.

The trees grew over big frames and leaned on wires. Their leaves rustled as they passed, and you could almost hear them growing: a stealthy rustling and whispering as tendrils uncoiled and groped and twisted.

There were insects in the forest: butterflies and bright-red beetles, and little flies with eyes like jewels and wings like lace. Gift loved them all.

There was a man walking ahead of them, and Gift didn't like him much. He wasn't Thorsgift, who Gift *did* like. They'd met him in the forest and he'd spoken to them angrily, saying: 'Why are you here?' Gift had hidden behind his mother.

His mother had said to the man, 'I'm here to talk with the Lady.'

The man hadn't liked that. He'd said, 'What lady? What are you talking about?'

Odinstoy had raised her hands, lifting them up as if imitating the upward growth of the thick stems and leaves around them. 'The Lady. You can hear her. You can hear the leaves rustle as she goes by.'

The man had said, 'What are you? Mad?'

'Yes,' Odinstoy had said, and laughed loudly. 'Mad, mad, mad!'

Then the man had started to laugh, and he'd said, 'You tell the truth!'

So now they were going with the man, and he was talking about the forest. Gift didn't understand a lot of what he said – Odinstoy said it was all about how many grapes would grow on each plant, and how much food and water the man gave the plants.

'I'm the God-speaker – Osbourne's God-speaker,' Odinstoy told the man, and the man looked surprised.

112

'We live Osbourne,' Gift told the man, and the man looked very impressed – so impressed that Gift felt shy again and hid behind his mother.

'That Aesir place,' the man said.

'I speak for Odin,' Odinstoy said.

'I'm for Zeus and all of them,' the man said.

Then Odinstoy stepped close to him, looked into his face, touched his arm and said, 'There is love for you.'

Gift watched as the man stepped back, looking startled, even shocked.

Odinstoy laughed again and said, 'The Lady loves you – you know the Lady?'

'What're you talking about?'

'About Our Mother.' When he looked still more confused, she said, 'The Mother of all of us.'

'Oh – Mother Earth?'

Odinstoy turned back to Gift, taking his hand. As they walked away, she said, 'He'll remember me.'

Affie stepped in and out of the shower again, and found the pale-blue dress that was the most flattering one she'd been given.

She looked into the mirror in the shower room while combing out her hair, and noted the bright-pink and even magenta and scarlet lights that flickered through it. She felt breathlessly excited. She was also remembering, and regretting, all the clothes she'd once owned, all the jewellery and make-up. Where did you get those things on Mars? Maybe Jason would know – he could take her on a spending spree. She badly needed so many things. Odinstoy must be being paid *something*. And she was her *wife*, wasn't she?

She went into a little reverie, where she imagined herself in all her favourite shops, somehow transplanted to Mars, buying a new wardrobe and perfume and skin creams. And nail-art. Facials. Massages. Everything she needed.

It made her forget, for a while, her nervousness about Jason arriving; but she *was* horribly nervous. What could she say? Would he like her, or think her silly? He had to think her pretty, but she wasn't looking her best.

When the doorbell rang, her heart hammered, her breath was short, but she jumped up, knowing it was Jason. She called out to the door to open, but her breath failed, and then her tongue tangled, and the computer couldn't understand her. In the end, she took the couple of steps to the door and pressed the button to open it herself. Outside stood a man's shirt. She looked up and saw Thorsgift looking down. The disappointment felt like a slap.

'Odinstoy?' Thorsgift said.

'She isn't here.'

'Oh. Is she by the pond? I didn't see her.'

Before Affie could answer, a voice from behind Thorsgift said, 'Hello! Do I have a rival?' Affie's heart soared.

Thorsgift shuffled aside and turned. There stood Jason, on the path, beaming, looking as handsome as he had ever done, and holding a large, brightly-striped paper bag. 'Is it a party?'

Affie was smiling foolishly. 'Thorsgift's come calling on Toy.' To Thorsgift, she said, 'I don't know where Toy is, or when she'll be back. Sorry.' She took a step back into the house, and Jason walked past Thorsgift, who watched him with a hard eye.

Jason threw himself down on the bench and put his bag beside him. Affie remained in the doorway, waiting for Thorsgift to go – but he was glaring at Jason.

Behind Affie, Jason unpacked his bag onto the table: a bottle of wine, a box of strawberries and another of chocolates. He sang lightly to himself: 'Ho-de-ho, hum-de-hum—'

Thorsgift stared, then looked down at Affie. 'What's going on? Who is he?'

'A friend,' Affie said. 'Do you want to join us, Thorsgift?'

'No. I wanted to see Odinstoy.'

'She isn't here, Thorsgift. I told you.'

'No,' Thorsgift agreed, while staring hard at Jason. 'But *he* is.' Then he turned his back and walked away.

Behind her, Jason laughed. Affie shut the door and turned to him, doubled over herself, her hand to her mouth, laughing.

'Ooooh!' Jason said, pointing. 'Oooh, you'll be in trouble, you will! Ooh, you naughty girl! It'll be all round the town in an hour.'

'What's his problem?' Affie asked.

'Well, my girl, you *are* a married woman, after all.'

Affie felt a little less like laughing. She found it hard to take seriously, despite everything, that she was supposed to be married to Odinstoy. At the back of her mind was always the notion that it was a game.

Jason was staring at her. 'You are every bit as beautiful as I remember. You don't seem real.'

Affie tingled with delight. 'I was designed,' she said.

'I know – by Hephastion. Only a God could design you.'

Hephastion was the Artist among the Gods, the Smith, the maker of their magical weapons, but also of the most delicate and magnificent jewellery for the Goddesses.

'If you keep saying things like that, I shall grow to like you,' Affie said. 'I'll find some glasses.'

She came back from the little kitchen with plates as well as glasses, and they occupied themselves with dividing up the strawberries. The silence between them was a little awkward. They kept glancing at each other, and smiling, and then fussing with the plates and fruit again. Jason opened the wine.

'You seemed worried,' he said, 'when we spoke earlier. What's the trouble?'

'Oh – it's not trouble exactly . . .' Affie dipped a strawberry in wine and ate it. It was sweet and rich. 'Oh! That's gorgeous!'

'From my family's farm,' Jason said. 'So's the wine.'

'Your family own a vineyard?' Affie said.

'You have to own land, don't you?' Jason said, taking

a sip from his glass. 'You're nothing but a bonder other-wise.'

Affie gazed at him, impressed. Not only did he come from a land-owning family, but he had such political insight!

'But what's troubling you?' Jason asked. He put down his glass and leaned towards her, looking deeply into her eyes. Such a shame his own were so small and squinty.

Affie's heart seemed to take a little tumble inside her chest. It was so lovely to find that someone cared about her and was keen to help her. She felt stronger, safer; and she wondered how she'd ever thought that Jason wasn't handsome.

'Tell me,' he said.

With a warm feeling of gratitude, she told him. 'Odinstoy's gone off and left me . . . And I don't have any money – or know where to buy things. I don't know why she's gone – we're supposed to be starting our lives here, and she's gone—'

Jason touched her arm. 'If that's all, you've nothing to worry about. I can let you have some money—'

'Oh, would you?' Affie looked at him, wide-eyed. This, she felt, was how things should be. People should help each other like this, and be kind and understanding.

'Of course. What do you need to buy?'

'So much . . . Clothes. Make-up. Shoes. Jewellery. Bags. I just need everything!'

'I've an idea,' Jason said. 'Why don't we go to Ares – you can stay at my place, or put up at a hotel if you prefer

– and we can take our time, look around, and buy you everything you need.'

Affie didn't need to answer. Her big, bright smile said yes for her.

A Marriage Proposal

The little machine trundled along the low wall to another spot, paused a moment, and then trundled on, making Gift shout with glee. Behind the machine, the wall began, magically, to grow in width and height.

At other places on the site, other machines were trundling along other low walls, which grew behind them. On all sides, buildings were growing as the machines tracked along the walls, paused, and moved on. Arching over the whole site, enclosing it, a part-dome was already in place.

'They're building the town for me, see,' Penny said. She held Gift's hand and pointed out the robots while Odinstoy stood beside her, watching and listening. 'Do you know how they know where to go?' Penny asked.

Gift, looking up into her face with his big, clear blue eyes, shook his head.

'They follow whiffy, pongy stinky trails! Pooh! Like sniffer-dogs.'

Gift laughed, jerking at her hand with amusement, and shouted, 'Stinky! Pooh!'

'That's right! And you know what the robots are doing? They're carrying lots and lots of other robots – tiny, teensy little robots – so small you can't see 'em.'

'Ha!' Gift shouted, in surprise, or disbelief.

'It's true. And every time a big robot stops, it's going *sploodge*!'

'*Sploodge!*'

'Yes, *sploodge* – and squirting out a bit of gunge. And that gunge is made up of chemicals, to make various things, and hundreds – thousands – of eeny-weeny robots. And all these eeny-weeny robots set to, and they make wall, and insulation and cables – oh, anything they're programmed to—'

'*Sploodge!* Pooh!' Gift laughed wildly.

'Yes,' Penny said. 'Pooh. Know what my job is? To watch them do it. Pooh.'

Gift laughed again. He liked Penny. He'd been tired and hungry when they'd first arrived here, after getting off the mono-rail. He'd dragged after Odinstoy, protesting and grizzling. Odinstoy had given him a biscuit from her pocket but after that had ignored him, apart from tugging him along.

Then they'd wandered into this new part-dome – Odinstoy had ducked under a striped rope and he'd followed after. They'd wandered among these unfinished but growing buildings, where the robots tirelessly trekked backwards and forwards, until Penny had come along, in her dark-blue clothes, and asked them if they were lost, adding, 'You shouldn't be here.'

Odinstoy had let go of Gift's hand, and hugged Penny as if she'd been a lost sister. 'There is love for you.'

Penny had staggered back from the hug, startled. 'I'm glad to hear it,' she'd said, 'but what are you doing here?'

'Hungry!' Gift had said. 'Hungry, me! Eat!'

Penny's eyes had flickered uncertainly to Odinstoy, who had smiled and said, 'It's a long time since we've eaten.'

The young woman, Penny, looked uncertain, then angry, then sad, and uncertain again. Finally, she sighed and said, 'Come on. I can give you something to eat. But then you have to go.'

She took them to a little plastic hut near the bubbles and hexagons of the dome wall. Inside there were a couple of plastic chairs and a desk with a computer. Notices and posters were stuck to the walls.

Penny made Odinstoy a coffee, apologising that she hadn't any milk or anything suitable for 'the little one' – but then was seized with inspiration and searched a filing cabinet, eventually producing a carton of blackberry-juice. From under the desk she brought a plastic box filled with biscuits, chocolate bars and small cakes, which made Gift's eyes grow big. From her own bag, she brought a box of sandwiches. Taking one for herself, she passed the rest to Odinstoy.

'I thank you,' Odinstoy said. 'Odin thanks you. And the Lady.'

Penny stared at her, attention suddenly arrested. She pointed. 'I've seen you. Weren't you – the new God-speaker somewhere?'

'I speak for Odin.'

'Yeah! I remember. I've seen you.' Penny stared at her, open-mouthed, rapt. 'You had a wife . . .'

'Odin wants me to speak for everyone, men and women. Husbands, wives, lovers, children. Bonders. Everyone.'

Penny went on staring, until Odinstoy reached out and rested her hand on the other woman's arm. 'What?'

'I'm . . . sort of interested in . . . that Aesir stuff.'

'In Odin?'

'Yeah,' Penny said, half-heartedly. 'But more . . . What are the others called?'

'Frey? Freya? Thor?'

'Thor, yeah! And – which one's the woman?'

'Freya.'

'Her, yeah. Them.' She stared at nothing until Odinstoy squeezed her arm, and then said, 'They just seemed – I dunno. Down to Earth. I was brought up to follow the True Gods—' She looked Odinstoy in the face and laughed. 'Sorry! I mean, you know, Zeus and Hera and Apollo, all them. And they just seem so spiteful and petty a lot of the time . . . I mean, more than they need be. But Freya and Thor, they seemed – more straightforward somehow. Fairer.'

'Thor, yes,' Odinstoy said. 'Freya, maybe. Odin is never straightforward.'

'I don't know much about Odin. But I'd like to know more about Thor and Freya.'

Odinstoy said, 'Freya means "The Lady" – did you know that?'

122

'No.'

'There's a new Lady coming. Odin has told me.'

Penny looked at her with a puzzled frown. She said, 'Yes?'

'Do you want to hear about Her – the new Lady?'

Penny was silent a moment, then said, 'Yes. I suppose – yes.'

Penny's gaze wandered, as it frequently had, to Gift, who was sitting on the floor of the hut, playing with the sweets and biscuits, eating some, and prattling to himself. Odinstoy, watching her, noted her expression and said, with certainty, 'The child will be born whole and safe, and it will be a boy.'

Penny's head snapped round. She gaped at Odinstoy, wide-eyed. 'I'm not even showing yet.'

'Odin told me.' She studied Penny's face. 'You're afraid.'

Penny laughed and shook her head, but then gulped. 'It's only natural, I suppose.'

Odinstoy went to her, crouched beside her chair and held her arms. 'There's no need to fear. Freya will be with you. Pray to Freya.'

Tears filled Penny's eyes. 'I've been praying to Artemis, and Hera – doesn't seem to help.'

She found herself held by Odinstoy's stare. She thought she'd never seen eyes so beautiful or so dark. 'You don't believe in them. Ask Freya to help you.'

'I don't know—'

'I'll help you.'

Odinstoy and Gift went home with Penny that night,

ate with her, slept at her house. After Gift was asleep, Penny sat with Odinstoy on the bench under her bed-space, and they talked and talked.

The next morning when they left, Odinstoy hugged Penny, kissed her, and said, 'Remember me.'

They tottered through the doors of the agency, giggling, clumsy with shopping bags. 'We want,' Jason sang out, high on espressos and spending, 'to see some bonders. Straight away!'

A receptionist at a highly-polished steel table looked startled and then put-out. She was probably free, Affie thought, but if her parents had designed her, they had it done cheaply. She was pretty, but very ordinary.

A young man rose from a table at the back of the room, murmuring, 'If you'd like to come this way, Frees . . .' Oh, how good it was to be addressed as 'Free' again; how important it was to be free! The young man they were following through into the back of the premises was almost certainly a bonder. His clothes were dark, neat, but cheap, ready-made stuff.

He led them through into a room furnished dully, but pleasantly, with gauze drapes and large flower arrangements. Three viewing screens stood at different points, with gilt-legged couches and chairs in front of them. 'Does this screen suit you, Frees?'

Jason threw himself onto the couch, dropping his bags beside it. 'Oh, get on with it!' Affie giggled as she collapsed beside him. 'The lady wants to buy a bonder!'

The young man sat on an upright chair. 'Certainly. May I ask if you have any specific skills or qualities in mind?'

'Oh – somebody who can cook, and look after my clothes, and do all that sort of thing,' Affie said.

'That should be no problem.' The young man pressed a button on his cuff, and the screen came on. 'Would you prefer a male or female?'

'I don't know—'

'You naughty gel, Aff,' Jason said.

'Let me see what you have,' Affie finished.

The young man pressed his sleeve again, and the screen filled with the agency's symbol and marching music played from the speakers. Affie settled back. She was feeling more relaxed and happy than she had since before she'd been bonded – exhausted from the excitement of shopping, sated with buying; and now she found that nothing made you feel richer and freer than viewing other people with the intention of buying them.

But the little potted biographies of the bonders hadn't lasted fifteen minutes before she felt disappointed. The women, even the young ones, all reminded her of Freda, the personal bonder she'd owned on Earth, when she'd been rich. Freda had been so old and drab, and so boring and annoying. She'd been sold on when Affie's father had killed himself and the good days had ended. Freda had been so scared . . .

'I don't like any of these,' Affie said.

The young man froze the screen. Jason looked at her.

'Can I show you another category?' the young man asked.

'You know what I'd like?' Affie said. 'Something like Pookie.' Her eyes filled with sudden tears, but both the men looked blank. 'Pookie was a pet I had on Earth. He was a cheetah – a miniature one – only about so high. He was silver with blue spots. *So* cute.'

They were still looking at her. 'What's a *cheeter*?' Jason asked.

'A kind of cat.'

'An animal?' said the young man. 'I'm afraid we don't deal in animals. Only people.'

'Do you know where I could get one? It doesn't have to be a cheetah. A leopard would do.'

'We could find you a cat,' Jason said, 'but I don't know about these *cheeters* and *lepods*.'

'I know!' Affie was struck by an idea. 'Do you have any children?' Children were small and cute, and bonder-children were tamed and good, not like Gift.

'Why, yes. A wide selection.' The bonder started the screen again.

The potted biographies started again, chuntering along, all accompanied by short films of coy, or smiling, or shyly-staring children; some pale-skinned and fair, some dark-skinned with curly or straight hair, some with brown or red hair, blue-eyed, brown-eyed, gap-toothed; some teenage—

'Too old,' said Affie, who was becoming clearer about what she wanted as she watched. 'I don't want one as old as me.'

'This is Boo,' wittered the soundtrack. 'Here is Charlie . . . Look at Mini's smile . . . Isn't Peri sweet?'

'That's all the children we have,' the young man said, eventually.

'Show them again – but just the white ones.'

'You should have a dark one,' Jason said. 'To match you.'

'I want a contrast – and I'm not very dark. So I want a little one, as pale as possible . . .'

The young man looked alert and pressed buttons on his sleeve. The screen flicked to a picture and froze on it. Captioned 'Boo', it showed a small, very pale boy, with large grey eyes, blue veins and red hair.

'Perfect!' Affie said. 'Can you have a set of clothes made for him? A little, you know –' she gestured about her own head – 'little green cap, little green jacket, green trousers, green shoes.'

'Certainly. It will be extra, of course.'

'Oh, of course,' Affie said. 'And some spare suits of clothes, too.'

The young man made notes on his wristband. 'Will you pay in full, or do you require credit?'

'Credit,' Affie said. 'When can you deliver?'

An hour later, the lift whisked them up to Jason's apartment. The door read his iris and opened for them and, laughing and talking noisily, they strolled through to the main room. Behind them came the doorman, carrying all their bags.

'Drop them there,' Jason said, 'and take yourself off.'

'Oh wonderful!' Affie kicked off her new shoes, which pinched a bit. It was so like the old times on Earth. It was as life should be.

A middle-aged man appeared at an inner doorway and stood there, his hands linked in front of him. He had a plump face, with deep folds between his nose and mouth. He was bald on top, and his remaining hair was cropped close. His clothes were all plain black.

'Oh Felix!' Jason said, and turned to Affie. 'My bonder. One of the best – I got him from the Olympus Agency. Had him years. Felix! Coffee now, certainly, and a little something to eat, I think. What is there?'

'Scones, sir. Or smoked salmon. Or cheese.'

'Affie, what do you fancy?'

It was so lovely to be asked such questions again. 'Ooh – scones!'

'Scones, then, Felix. And Felix – there's going to be a delivery this evening. A bonder – Affie bought him this afternoon. Can you look after him?'

'Of course, sir.' Felix gave a deep nod and left the room.

Affie was looking around, taking in her surroundings for the first time since they'd tumbled through the door. She almost nodded in approval. It was the largest, finest living-space she'd seen since leaving Earth – and the most like an Earth apartment. It was large, and in the best position – high enough to be above the noise of the streets, but not so high that it was among the gantries and creaking of the dome.

The walls were of a dull, metallic gold, with panels of red and green copper; the floor was of slate-grey tiles. They were half sitting, half lying at either end of a large, chocolate-brown sofa, and there were other chairs hanging from the ceiling.

A small forest of shrubs and plants, growing in pots and tubs of various shapes and colours, filled one corner. A large viewing screen almost filled one wall. 'Command,' Jason said. 'Music.' Soft music, flowing and rippling like water, came whispering from hidden speakers, while the screen filled with changing colours: soft blues, greens, pinks, like out-of-focus flowers.

'This is a lovely place,' Affie said.

Jason looked round himself. 'It's not bad, but we have better . . . You should see our place out at Olympus, and the one by the lakes. I shall have to take you to see them.'

Affie felt as if there was a small, gently-warmed pot nestling just under her breastbone. The warmth spread through her, a lovely, thrilling sensation. This place was OK, but she should see their other places! And he was going to take her to see them!

Oh, her luck was changing! Her life had been horrible lately, knocked off its proper tracks, tipping her into all sorts of grime and thistles. But now she was raised up again and cruising on her way . . .

Felix returned with a tray of coffee and scones, set it on a low table and left. Affie hardly noticed, she was so absorbed in unpacking shoes, blouses, skirts, underwear, jackets, dresses, and draping them over the sofa. Buying them had been a delight, but as she unpacked them, a sickness settled on her heart.

'What's the matter?' Jason asked. He was like that: so attentive, quick to notice any little change in her mood.

'Odinstoy's going to be so angry.'

'Why? Don't you deserve some new things?'

'Yes, but I didn't ask, and – the bonder was so expensive.'

'Do you have to ask?' He sounded surprised.

Affie sat suddenly among all her new clothes. 'Oh Jason – I'm frightened of her!' She glanced sidelong at him, hoping for sympathy.

He leaned towards her. 'Frightened?'

'She hits me. If I do anything she doesn't like, she shouts and hits me.'

Jason took her hands and stroked them.

Affie said, 'I wish I'd never married her!'

'So do I,' Jason said, 'because then you could marry me.'

The sand was reddish, and people lay on it everywhere, on brightly-coloured towels or airbeds. Children ran about, dug, wailed.

The beach sloped gently down to a blue sea, where polite little waves bobbed into shore. There were paddlers and swimmers, and children crouching at the water's very edge.

High above, the sun shone down through the bubbles of the dome, scattering rainbows. Gulls screamed, mothers screamed, ice-cream sellers screamed. Odinstoy sat, hugging her knees and looking out, curiously, to where the curved walls of the domes came down into the water. Did the domes completely enclose the lake, she wondered, or did the water go on beyond the walls? She couldn't see a beach on the other side.

She made sure she knew where Gift was – he was organising some children nearby to dig a hole – and then shuffled over to the family on a nearby carpet of towels.

'Hi, I'm Odinstoy – can I ask you something?'

A woman looked round, startled at suddenly being addressed by a stranger, but she squinted and smiled in a friendly fashion.

'I'm from Earth,' Odinstoy said. 'Can you tell me – does the lake end before the wall? Or does the wall go down to the bottom of the lake?'

The woman was baffled and looked round for help. A boy of about fifteen, who sat beside her, said, 'The walls go down below the waterline, and they're bolted into the rock – that way, the water can come in, but the atmosphere's sealed out.'

'Thanks,' Odinstoy said.

'Are you here on holiday?' the woman asked.

'I'm Osbourne's new God-speaker,' Odinstoy said.

The woman and boy both looked blank.

'I speak for Odin.'

'Who's Odin?' the boy asked. A girl, behind him, propped herself up on her elbow to listen.

Odinstoy told of Odin: of how He brought wisdom;

how He gave mankind mead; how He foresaw the end of the world. As she talked, Gift came, and pressed close to her.

The family listened politely, a little bored, a little resentful. 'We're Church of Mars,' the mother said. 'Want a sandwich?'

Gratefully taking one, and giving one to Gift, Odinstoy said, 'You are children of Odin.'

And when she and Gift had eaten several sandwiches and biscuits and plastic cups of juice, she said, 'Shall I read the runes for you?'

'We're C of M,' the mother said. 'No thank you.'

'You're a good woman,' Odinstoy said, 'with a beautiful family –' the woman's face brightened '– whatever Gods you follow. Remember Odinstoy.'

The woman looked half minded to laugh. The boy, glancing round at his sister, did snigger.

'Remember Odinstoy. When you hear of the Lady, Odin's Queen, remember Odinstoy.' She stood and took Gift's hand. 'We'll go home now.'

'Affie?' Gift said.

'Affie.'

As they walked away, the boy, behind them, said, 'Remember Odinstoy!' His mother and sister laughed. But they did remember.

'You mean it?' Affie gasped. It was so exactly what she wanted that it seemed unreal.

'I need a wife,' Jason said, 'and you're perfect. No one

could be more beautiful. And you know how to behave – who is your family?'

He was speaking a language Affie recognised. A man needed a wife, as he needed a car and a house, and he chose one in much the same way. A happy smile was on her face, but words caught in her throat. 'They're – oh – they're on Earth.'

'Yes, of course, but we know some of the Earth families . . . Why did they send you to Mars?'

'They didn't! They—' A good idea came to her. 'They didn't approve of me marrying Odinstoy – and they were right. It was a mistake.'

He nodded. Her heart turned over with thankfulness and relief. He understood.

'But who are your family? I might have heard of them.'

'The Millingtons.' Disappointingly, he showed no sign of having heard of them. 'We're a good family. Had property . . . If we were in Osbourne, I could show you my ancestors.'

'I'd be interested to see them.'

Affie waited, half expecting that he would show her his ancestor tree. She even glanced round to see where it was. Instead, he said, 'I suppose your family disapproved of Odinstoy because she was a bonder.'

He was coming so close to the truth that Affie felt cold. 'And because she spoke for Odin. They just didn't like her at all.' Nor would they have done, if they'd ever met her.

Jason moved close to her and put his arm along the

back of the chair behind her. Affie's nervousness increased, but she was also thrilled because it seemed he liked her.

'Families,' he said, his head close to hers. 'Aren't they a pain?'

Affie giggled, more because his breath was tickling her, and his hand was on her shoulder, than because of any amusement she felt.

'Pretty colours in your hair,' he said. 'You know, my people have been on at me for ages to marry, but until I saw you, I wasn't interested.'

Affie's breathing was quick and fast; and she was thrilled to the core.

'I got into awful trouble once,' Jason said. 'You know what I did?'

Affie stared at him at close quarters, at his thick dark lashes, his thick dark brows. 'No. What?'

'I stole a vase from one of my parents' friends. I didn't even want it! What would I want with a vase? But I was bored, and I saw it, and I just liked it – liked the colours – it was glass, a sort of pearly blue. So I put it in my pocket – it was small – and took it. Then my mother came across it in my room months later. Oh dear, the fuss! Laughable, really. Turns out it was really rare and valuable, and my mother's friend had missed it. She'd actually sent one of her bonders back because she thought the girl had taken it.'

Affie felt a cold spasm pass through her. She could imagine what it would have been like to be that bonder, protesting her innocence to an angry employer and not being believed – and then returned to her agency with a black mark against her. Thank Zeus – or Odin, or whoever she was meant to thank these days – that she wasn't a bonder any more.

And then she thought: But I am. I'm only pretending not to be. I might be found out.

'I've never told anyone else that,' Jason said, and looked into her eyes.

Affie's heart opened like a rose. She was special to him. She had to let him know that he was special too.

'I wish I'd met you before I married Odinstoy,' she said. She giggled, a little wildly. 'But then I'd never have come to Mars, and I'd never have met you!'

Still looking into her eyes, Jason said, 'Life is really strange sometimes.'

Gazing back into his little black eyes, Affie thrilled at those words. That is so true, she thought. Life really is strange sometimes. It was wonderful to meet someone who understood things like that.

'A marriage is easy enough to end,' he said.

She felt a little shaky.

'How?'

'In Osbourne? It's easier there than anywhere because they're almost all Aesirian. You just make a declaration before witnesses, I think. Something really simple anyway. Then you'd be free to marry me.'

She looked at him. 'You're not teasing me? You really, truly want to marry me?'

He nodded. 'And look after you, and make you happy. But Affie—'

'Yes.'

'I have to know everything about you. I have to know what I'm taking on. I don't want any surprises afterwards. So, if there's anything I should know . . .'

'Well,' Affie said. And then she told him.

She didn't mean to tell him much, at first. Only that her father had got into debt and killed himself – because, if he looked into her background, he might find that out for himself, and at least it let him know that she *did* come from a good family, who once had money and property, and only lost it through bad luck.

But then it seemed that she had to tell him that she'd been sold – because he would want to know what happened after her father's death, and she couldn't make a story up all in a moment. And his face showed such concern for her, and he put his arms round her and cuddled her, while stroking her back. That was so nice, being cuddled, being loved. She relaxed into his arms, almost drinking up the closeness, feeling herself dissolve in softness.

'Oh, that must have been so hard for you,' he said, so kindly, while his hands stroked, and she started to cry. The rest of the story poured out with her tears – how she'd been sold to the Perrys, and how she'd met Odinstoy, and how Odinstoy had agreed to bring her to Mars if she'd steal the little boy from the Perrys' house, because he was really Odinstoy's little boy by Perry.

'Oh, poor you,' he said, stroking her back with his warm hand. 'Poor, poor you.'

Affie pulled away from him. She had a horrible feeling that she'd done something she shouldn't. 'Don't hate me.'

'Hate you? I admire you. It must have taken a lot of courage.'

Affie smiled.

'I'm so glad you told me, Affie. I feel honoured. I'm proud that you feel you could be so honest with me.'

Affie's spirit recovered and blossomed a little more with each word.

'I'll never tell anyone else,' Jason said. 'Not before or after your divorce, not before or after our wedding.' And he kissed her.

Odin's Gathering

Thorsgift had been working on the accounts for his family's land; but it was a Thursday, the day sacred to his name-God, Thor. On that day he always took a long dinner break. After eating, he would go to his ancestor shrine – a screen hanging in a corner, on which he could call up a family tree, photographs, film-clips, wills and marriage records, birth certificates. Sensing his approach, the screen came to life and displayed: first, a family tree, and then, at random, a short film of a smiling woman – his great-grandmother. There was a shelf under the screen, and on it he set down the plate of small cakes he'd brought as an offering, together with a glass. Under his arm he carried a bottle of wine, and from it he filled the glass, before lighting the candles. Setting the bottle on the floor, he held up his hands, palms towards the screen, and said a small prayer of thanks to all his ancestors, asking them to go on watching over him and the rest of his family. Under his breath, he said to them, 'You know how I feel about Odinstoy . . .' He didn't say any more. The ancestors only needed a hint. They saw into his heart. If there was anything to be done, any influence they could bring, they would do it. He bowed to them, said goodbye, and left the house to walk to Thor's shrine.

He went there every Thursday, to make an offering to the God and pray. He could expect to meet other people who'd been named for Thor, and things might develop into shared worship, or just a good old natter.

It was as he left his house that he saw Odinstoy, and stopped short in surprise. She was carrying Gift, and was struggling with the task, constantly shifting him from arm to arm, and pausing while she hoisted him higher. It wasn't surprising – Gift was a solid, heavy child and Odinstoy a small woman.

Thorsgift hurried towards her, calling to her. She stopped again and looked round, but his walk slowed as he remembered calling on Affie and seeing her with that strange man. And Affie had been absent from the village for several days too, though she was back now – Inga Curtis had seen her arrive, the day before, in a taxi with many bags and, amazingly, a small boy. An oddly-dressed small boy, at that. There had been much discussion and speculation, by e-mail, and phone, and around the duck-pond. Where had Affie been, and why? Who was the man she'd left with? Could the boy possibly be a bonder? What was Odinstoy going to say to that?

Thorsgift wondered if he should mention the strange man, or the boy. There was a risk of making Odinstoy angry – but maybe she needed to know. He couldn't make up his mind and so called out, with slightly false cheeriness, 'Good to see you again! When did you get back?'

'Carry Gift for me,' Odinstoy said. 'He's tired. We've walked a long way.'

Gift was asleep, or close to it. Thorsgift took the child from her, happy to show how much stronger he was than her, how much help he could be. 'Why didn't you take the mono or a taxi?'

'No credit,' Odinstoy said.

Thorsgift frowned. He knew that she was being paid by the gathering – not a huge amount, but then, from what he'd seen she didn't spend much either. But according to Inga, Affie had been carrying an awful lot of expensive-looking bags, so maybe it wasn't too hard to guess where all the credit had gone.

He had to say something. Affie could ruin everything by going on spending sprees and running about with men instead of playing the part of God-speaker's wife. If they were found out, Odinstoy would be in terrible trouble – and so would he, since he'd helped them. Theft of a bonder. Kidnapping of a child. These weren't trivial charges.

'Odinstoy—' he began seriously, but then someone else called out their names. Rebecca was coming over to them.

'Odinstoy,' she said, extending both hands, 'where *have* you *been*? We've been quite worried about you.'

'Travelling,' Odinstoy said. 'With Odin.'

'Oh,' Rebecca said. 'Well, we're glad to have you back.'

'I'm glad to be back. I have things to tell you.'

'Really?' Rebecca linked arms with Odinstoy as she

walked on. Thorsgift followed, carrying Gift. 'Me person-
ally, or—?'

'Everyone,' Odinstoy said. 'I want everyone to come
to the gathering. Odin has news for you.'

'That's exciting!' Rebecca exclaimed. 'I am so pleased
– and relieved – because, to be truthful, I'd been asked to
have a word with you, and—'

'Because I've been away?' Odinstoy asked.

'Well . . . People were wondering—'

'Why they're paying me when I'm not here?'

'I wasn't going to say that,' Rebecca said.

Odinstoy stopped and yanked her arm from Rebecca's
hold. Facing the woman, she said, 'But it's what everyone's
been saying, and thinking. Did they stop my credit?'

'What?'

'Did you stop my credit because I wasn't here, at your
beck and call – like a bonder?'

Rebecca, her mouth open, stepped back from the anger
in Odinstoy's voice and face, in her very posture. 'I – Well
– I don't know about that.'

Thorsgift, stooping near, said quietly, warningly,
'Odinstoy, I—'

She struck out at him, making Rebecca flinch. 'Who
owns my bond?' Odinstoy demanded. 'Who is my master?
Who?'

Rebecca took another step back, looking round for
some excuse to break off this awkward conversation.

'Odin! I am Odin's bonder! I run to no one else's call!
I speak for Odin, not for you! Tell them that! And tell

them to be at the next gathering. Odin orders it. He has word for them.'

'Ah. Yes. Well,' Rebecca said. 'I'll speak to you another time, I think. Good sol!' And she walked away, her face rather red.

'Odinstoy,' Thorsgift said. 'You shouldn't speak to her like that.'

She swung round on him, and he dodged away, hugging her heavy child to his chest, fearing she was going to attack him. 'Are *you* Odin?' she demanded.

'No, but—'

'Then don't tell me what I can do!'

She walked on towards her house, and he followed, carrying Gift. 'Odinstoy, they didn't stop your credit. I would have heard.'

'It's stopped!'

'Odinstoy . . . I have to tell you this . . . Affie's been away to Ares. With a man. She came back yesterday, with lots of shopping bags. And a little boy.'

Odinstoy stopped and stared at him.

'It's true,' he said. 'Everyone knows.'

'What man?'

'Nobody knows who he is.' He thought about telling her that he had, briefly, met him, but decided against it. 'He wasn't from Osbourne, and he's not in the gathering. Odinstoy, if Affie – if she starts a lot of trouble, she'll get us *all* into it.' He looked at her hard.

Odinstoy stood very still, looking away from him, staring at nothing.

'Odinstoy—'

'I'm thinking!' After a few more moments, she said, 'Give me back Gift.'

She took the child back from him, bracing herself against the weight, and walked away. Thorsgift watched her go, and then walked to the Thor shrine. It was in one of Osbourne's outlying half-domes. A large oak tree, the tree sacred to Thor, grew at its centre, and the shrine was beneath it. An old figure of the God, carved from red Martian stone, showed him smiling and bearded, grasping a hammer that rose from his hips. On the ground around it, in the grass and fallen leaves and acorns, were candles and lanterns, and offerings: cakes, loaves, bowls of milk and beer. From the low branches of the tree hung prayers in bottles, ribbons, scraps of cloth. Thorsgift took a cake from his pocket and put it on the stone ledge carved into the statue's plinth. He raised his hands and prayed, for the fortune of Osbourne and its people, for his own family, and for Odinstoy. As an afterthought, he threw in one for Affie. 'Thor, she needs Your special protection.'

Affie felt clear about one thing only: she hated being back in the cramped little cage at Osbourne. Even more cramped with Boo taking up space.

She hadn't wanted to come back. Jason's apartment had been so beautiful and comfortable, with so much space, and a bathroom with water, and a bonder who was a lot more useful than Boo had turned out to be. 'If we're going to be married, why don't I just stay here?' she'd asked. 'It'd be easier.'

He'd insisted that it would cause far too much trouble. She wasn't divorced yet, and she'd have to go back to Osbourne for that; and he hadn't yet spoken to his family. Why give spiteful people something to gossip about? Besides, he'd have to go out to Olympus to see his family, so she'd be left on her own. Better go home.

'I could come with you,' she said. 'You told me you'd show me the place.'

'It's better I see my people by myself first. I can ask advice about your divorce. Later on, when that's all in hand, then you can meet them.'

'I'll stay here, then,' Affie had said, looking round. She really wouldn't have minded having that flat to herself, with Felix to look after her.

'Felix will be coming with me,' Jason said; and had overborne all her other protests. So she'd had to come back, unwillingly, to Osbourne.

It was a miserable place, seeming tinier than ever, with hardly room to take a deep breath. And so inconvenient! Boo, it turned out, could just about make a hot drink so, if she wanted to eat, she had to go to all the bore of cooking for herself, or just eating depressing things, like dry bread and cold apples. And feed Boo as well! He looked very pretty in his green clothes, and she'd been delighted when he'd been delivered to Jason's flat, but in Osbourne she quickly found his wide-eyed but baleful stare annoying.

Her worn clothes lay where she'd thrown them the night before. 'Can you do laundry?' she asked Boo. He stared. 'I mean, clean clothes – can you?' Another long stare, and then a slight shake of the head. 'Oh, what use are you!' She felt extreme boredom at the thought that she'd have to pick up the clothes, and clean them and put them away herself. It would be just like being a bonder again. How could she think of important things, like her divorce from Odinstoy, and becoming a famous fashion designer, when there were so many irritating, petty, boring little jobs to do? That was what bonders were for: to relieve you of all these nasty little chores.

She was startled by the click of the door-lock releasing. The door opened and Odinstoy came in, leading Gift by the hand.

Affie blinked at them. Though they'd been separated for a matter of days, it suddenly seemed like weeks; and though she recognised them both at once, they also seemed like strangers. Gift was such a big child for his age: more like eight than four, and she was surprised to see what a bonny child he was, with glassily-clear blue eyes, rosy cheeks and flaxen hair.

Odinstoy, small and dark, seemed the last person to be his mother. If she hadn't known better, Affie would have supposed her to be his bonder-nanny.

Boo, startled by the sudden entrance of these strangers, huddled against the door of the kitchen, where he was standing, and stared at Affie, as if asking what he should do.

145

Odinstoy looked at him, and the bags lying on the floor, without comment or expression; while Gift looked round with curiosity.

Jumping up, Affie said, 'Oh! You're back!' She felt as if she'd been caught in the middle of some wicked act.

Odinstoy threw herself onto the bench, drawing Gift to sit beside her. 'We're back. What is there to eat?'

'Not much,' Affie said, feeling still more uncomfortable. She edged in front of Boo, as if to hide him. Odinstoy was going to say that she should have bought food, which was *so* unfair.

'What's all this?' Odinstoy kicked one of the bags.

'Nothing,' Affie said, snatching at bags, and wishing that putting the things away hadn't seemed such a tedious chore. Moving to pick them up left Boo in plain view again, but Odinstoy seemed to be ignoring him – which made Affie afraid.

Odinstoy took up another of the bags and unpacked from inside it a pair of high-heels, a pair of boots, and a necklace. Looking at Affie, she said, 'Nothing?'

Affie felt as if she was being scalded.

Odinstoy took up another bag and emptied it of a heap of clothing: three skirts, two tops and a jacket.

In a third bag were several different kinds of make-up in fancy, pretty little pots; two boxes holding earrings; several packs of hosiery and several matching sets of underwear.

Odinstoy looked straight at Boo and said, 'Who are you?'

He tried to speak, but swallowed the sound.

Odinstoy looked at Affie. 'Who is he?'

'Well,' Affie began, thinking she would simply explain, quite calmly, how she came to buy Boo . . . But she ran out of words.

Odinstoy looked at Boo again. She studied him for a few moments, without any expression, and then held out her hand to him. He hesitated, then went over and stood beside her. 'This is my little boy,' Odinstoy said. 'He's called Gift. What's your name?'

'Boo.'

She pulled a face. 'That's the sort of stupid name people give to bonders. What's your real name?'

A sudden smile came to his face, then vanished, to be replaced by wariness.

Odinstoy put her hand on his shoulder and stroked it. 'I used to be a bonder. I was called "Kylie" then. Stupid name. Now I'm not a bonder any more, I call myself "Odinstoy".'

The boy's head jerked up. 'Odinstoy?'

Affie looked at him in surprise. It sounded just as if he'd heard of Odinstoy.

Odinstoy nodded. 'Yes. I'm Odinstoy. What's your name?'

'John.'

'Pleased to meet you, John,' Odinstoy said, and pulled him to lean against her. She looked at Affie. 'Now I know why my credit was stopped. And why I had to make Gift walk so far.'

'I needed a few basics,' Affie said.

'Necklaces? Earrings? A boy?'

'You begrudge me a few things?'

Odinstoy opened the boxes holding the necklace and earrings and threw them on the floor. 'Are we going to *eat* these?' Gift moved to the back of the bench, against the wall, and Boo – or John – withdrew into a corner, his face grimacing.

Odinstoy threw the boots on top of the jewellery. 'Is *Gift* going to eat these?'

Affie wanted to say that her new, stylish boots were good enough to eat, but far too nice to be fed to that brat. She wanted to ask why it was always Gift – Gift Gift Gift – that mattered. The words rose into her mouth, but fear made her choke on them.

So she wrenched her feelings into another track, lowered her head and her eyes and said, meekly, 'Odinstoy, perhaps it would be best if – I mean, we both have what we want now, don't we? You have Gift, and I'm free. We don't need to stay together any more, do we? I'm sure you and Gift would be happier without me and—'

'You want a divorce,' Odinstoy said.

Affie was relieved. Odinstoy had always been quick; but to guess so readily must mean that she'd been thinking the same. 'Yes,' Affie said, smiling.

'Who is he?'

Affie felt her face turn hot. 'Who?'

'The man, you bone-headed little cow, the man you've been with.'

'There's no—'

Odinstoy stood suddenly, and Affie backed hurriedly against the wall. Boo flinched. Only Gift was sure that he wouldn't be hurt.

'All right, OK!' Affie said. 'I met him at that party. He's really nice—'

'He says he's going to marry you?'

'Well – not *immediately*. He has to talk to his family first and then, of course—'

'His family?'

'They have a place out at Olympus and an apartment—'

'You shag him?'

Affie didn't answer, but looked about, frustrated all over again at how tiny the place was. There was nowhere she could go to get away from this uncomfortable discussion, except the tiny kitchen, and the tiny shower room – neither of them really an escape.

'Did you shag him?'

'I don't think that's any—'

'Did. You. Shag—'

'Yes! All right! I did! So what?'

Odinstoy threw herself down on the bench again. 'And you think he's going to marry you!'

A tremor of rage passed through Affie, sending a flush to her face. Pink and scarlet lights moved through her hair; her body shook. 'What would you know, you bonder?'

Odinstoy pointed at her and laughed. 'Short memory! You're a bonder too!'

Affie's rage grew even hotter. Her hair sparkled with bright-red lights, making Boo stare. She had to struggle for breath before she could speak. 'I'm *not*. A bonder. Any more!'

'But you're poor! You're not a rich little girl now. You don't have a rich family. You don't have houses and land. The only thing you have, you've already given him! So why should he marry you?'

'He will he will he will!'

Odinstoy stood and came to her with open arms. Affie, furious, turned away, but when Odinstoy touched her arm it was as if Affie's body turned by itself into Odinstoy's embrace. It was so wonderful, and comforting, to be offered a hug when she'd been expecting a blow. 'Never mind,' Odinstoy said. 'Hush now, hush.' When Affie had calmed a little, Odinstoy said, 'Come over here.'

She pulled Affie over to the computer screen set in the wall and, touching the screen, called up the programme that cast the runes. 'Choose one card,' Odinstoy said.

Still encircled by Odinstoy's arm, Affie reached out and touched the screen. The runes rose, circled, sank, rose again until one rune came to the fore and settled, filling the screen.

'Grave,' Odinstoy said, naming it.

Affie looked at her, alarmed.

'Your old life, your Earth life, is dead,' Odinstoy said. 'In its grave. You can't get it back.'

Affie shook her head, tears in her eyes.

'Grieve for it – but give it up. You're here, now – on Mars! Make a new life!'

But I want to! Affie thought. She was planning to. But if she could marry a rich man, like Jason, it would make it all so much easier. She'd have a nice home, and nice things, while she was becoming a famous fashion designer. 'I'm trying!'

'You *can't* have your old life back. It's gone.'

'If I marry Jason—'

'You'll be your husband's toy. You'll have to ask him for money. The money won't be yours. It'll be his. Maybe he'll give you a treat if you've pleased him – like a child. Or a pet animal. Or a bonder. Why are you so keen to make yourself into a bonder again?'

Affie had no answer but stood looking at the floor, stubbornly refusing to give up her hopes. I'd be a rich bonder, she thought. I'd be a bonder with beautiful clothes.

'Do something for me,' Odinstoy said. When Affie didn't answer, she shook her slightly. 'Send some mails for me. Send one to your friend, Leander. To the radio and the blogs. I'm calling a gathering. Odin has news for Mars.'

Affie didn't want to be interested. She wanted to be despondent. But she raised her eyes.

'Send the mails, wife,' Odinstoy said. 'Call them all in. Say, Odin calls a gathering. Odin has something to tell them.' She smiled. 'Want to know what it's about? Want to know before anybody else?'

Affie half turned away. Why should she be interested?

But her curiosity flickered. With a shrug she said, 'All right.'

'Odin's getting married,' Odinstoy said, and laughed again. 'Poor old sod – He's taking a wife.'

Odin's Queen

John – he was even beginning to think of himself as 'John' now, instead of 'Boo' – crouched in the darkness, holding the drumstick ready. He was so scared and excited that he had to keep shifting his grip on the stick and wiping his hands on his trousers, and his heart was thumping hard. It was an important job he had to do, in front of all these people, and he had to get it right.

'When everybody's in,' Odinstoy had told him, 'we'll turn off all the lights and make 'em wait ... Make 'em wait in the dark. And you beat the drum. Let 'em feel Odin coming.'

The gathering was in Osbourne's town hall, and it was full. He could hear them in the dark, sighing, breathing, scuffling, coughing. They were waiting ... They'd been waiting for a long time. John was aching to start drumming, but Odinstoy had told him to stay quiet until she signalled. If Odinstoy said wait, he would wait. He'd wait until he turned into a skeleton, with dust dripping off it – and even then, when she gave the signal, he'd beat the drum. He'd do anything for her.

When she'd told him her name, it had been like a jolt going through him, like a buzz of electricity. He'd heard of her. When he'd been in the agency's home, before Affie had bought him, the tutors and some of the older bonders had been talking about her. They said she was a witch; that she was possessed by an old, mad God. But they admired her too, you could tell that. They admired her because she was upsetting people. 'She'll make the fat cats sweat,' somebody had said. John knew that 'the fat cats' were the rich people, the owners, the people who bought them.

They said that, when she'd first set foot on Mars, she'd walked past all the rich people, and hugged and kissed a bonder. 'She used to be a bonder,' they said. 'She knows what it's like.' And, 'She says there shouldn't be any bonders. She says her God says there should be no bonders.'

That had started an argument. Some of the tutors had said, oh yes, and what are we all going to do, if there are no bonders? Who's going to house you and feed you if they have to pay you? Have you seen the way some Frees live? You're better off as a bonder, if you only knew.

John didn't know who was right about all that. He knew that he didn't like being a bonder, and having to work when he saw other children playing; and he thought anyone who said bonders should be freed must be a good person. And then he'd met Odinstoy, which he never thought he would, because she was sort of famous, and he'd never thought he would meet anyone famous. And she had been so *nice*.

She'd been very angry with Affie for buying him (and although Affie was the most beautiful lady he'd ever seen, he didn't like her much). He'd expected Odinstoy to be angry with him too, but she wasn't. She'd called him to her, and put her arm round him, just as she'd had her arm round the boy who was her own son. And she'd said 'Boo' was the sort of stupid name people give to bonders (which he knew was true), and had asked him what he'd wanted to be called. And he'd said, 'John', because he'd always, secretly, wanted to be called 'John'. It was such a plain, square, *good* name. It was never given to bonders. And Odinstoy had called him John from then on. She never forgot.

And she'd cooked for him, and given him some of her son's clothes to wear – Gift's clothes were a little too big, even though he was younger than John. She'd let him play with Gift, and hadn't asked him to do any real work – apart from asking him to pass her things, or pick up toys – the sort of work that any mother might ask her son to do. In a few more days, John thought, when they knew each other even better, he might find the nerve to ask if he could call her 'mother'. She might even say yes. She was wonderful.

The gathering were tiring of the wait. He could tell by the increase of foot shuffling and stamping, by the whispering that turned into quiet chatting . . . Had he missed the signal, let Odinstoy down?

Maybe he should begin. He wanted to begin. This waiting almost hurt. The quiet chatting was becoming ever louder talk. Someone nearby said, 'Why are we standing here in the dark?'

From the button pinned to his coat came Odinstoy's whisper: 'John! Now!'

He brought the stick down on his drum in three great blows: *BLAM! BLAM! BLAM!* Amplified, the blows crashed from the speakers, and brought a shocked silence.

Wait again, Odinstoy had said. Wait until they start to whisper again.

This time the waiting was easier. He was grinning to himself. When everyone started recovering from the shock, and giggling and whispering, he began to beat the drum steadily, not too loud at first.

The silence spread slowly this time. Those who heard the drum-beat fell quiet, and then others could hear it, and they were quiet, and so on until the whole gathering, standing in darkness, were silent, and only the drum could be heard.

Beat it like your heartbeat, Odinstoy had said, so John took up that rhythm, following the drubbing of his own heart, which was rather faster than usual. It had an effect. The gathering grew quiet, holding its collective breath – and something else seemed to press into the hall. He could feel it, leaning over him and everyone, pressing against him, filling the spaces between people. He could feel someone standing close by his right side – and the drum-beat faltered as he flinched and turned to look. There was no one there.

The gathering stirred and sighed. A light had appeared in the darkness at the back of the stage. John kept up the drum-beat as he looked over his shoulder to see it.

The light was round and glowing, a soft pearly light. It was carried, a small Earth's moon, by a dark figure, seen only as a dark shape behind the light. The figure held the light at arm's length as it came forward, slowly, and then stood still, centre-stage, holding out the softly-glowing globe.

John, as he had been instructed, gave three, final, smashing blows to the drum.

Silence. The many people of the gathering, even the children, stood completely still, holding their breath. What they were hearing and seeing was the more powerful for its simplicity. There was no film, no computer effects, no taped professional music . . . Just a drum-beat striking against their ears, reverberating in their bones; and a real darkness – not filmed and seen on a screen in a lit room – but a real darkness that enveloped them and blinded their eyes, and a real light that brought relief, breaking through the blindness. It was mesmerising.

The dark figure brought the light close to its body, so that it shone upward into the face – and the crowd moaned at the hideousness of that face – and then sighed with relief, even giggled, at the realisation that the light was shining on the folds of a dark veil draped over the figure's head.

But the face was uncovered – first the chin, then the nose and closed eyes – as the veil slithered from it, perhaps pulled from behind by someone unseen, but the impression, to the gathering, was that the veil moved by itself, unveiling.

The uncovered face, lit from below, was, at first, unrecognisable; but it was Odinstoy, her eyes closed. She stood perfectly still, her face lit from beneath by the glowing ball in her hands. She said nothing, didn't move, for a long, long time. She made them wait. And they waited. They hushed children, stifled coughs. If they grew impatient, then they stifled that too. They waited to hear Odin speak.

From Odinstoy's mouth came a man's voice: 'Well come, all those who came to my call. You shall be rewarded.'

There was the barest of stirrings and whispers from the crowd, quickly stilled as they listened again.

'I have been walking here on Mars,' Odin said, and another suppressed thrill ran through the crowd. 'I have been talking to the people of Mars, and to Mars.'

Odinstoy was silent a moment, then dropped the lamp she held to the floor, with a crash that made some jump and cry out. The lamp rolled to the side of the stage where it continued to light Odinstoy, faintly, from one side.

'I will ask you a question,' Odin said. 'Why do you worship Mother Earth? Why do you worship Earth when you are not on Earth, nor of Earth?'

The question was left to hang in the darkness. Everyone could feel the giant leaning close by their right shoulder. The hair rose on their skin. Many turned to look and half saw other people, dim in darkness; and heard their breaths.

The man's voice broke out again from the stage. 'I am here to give you a new mother, a greater mother, a richer mother—'

Odinstoy pulled apart the long robe she wore, and it fell to the ground, leaving her naked.

There was a brief, sharp outcry from the gathering; and a rustling and shuffling, of many people moving at once, turning to each other, pointing – then silence again.

From the naked woman came a man's voice. 'This is my Queen, my love, my chosen one. She and I shall be one, Sky and Mars. Come to the wedding! Come you all, and witness my promise – that I shall love her and guard her, and all of you, all of her children, shall be in our care, shall flourish, shall grow strong—'

There was a ground swell of snatched and released breaths, of sighs and groans, and whispers.

'I am Mother Mars!' The woman's voice rose sweetly above it all, in the darkness. 'I am your mother, I am Mother Mars!' She chanted it, her voice and her arms rising exultantly.

And, in the crowd, people began to whisper, to chant, 'Mother Mars! Mother Mars!'

'There is love for you!' Mother Mars cried out. 'Come to me, come to me! There is love for you!'

With a clatter of feet, a small figure dashed onto the stage – it was John, who had been the bonder, Boo. He ran to Odinstoy and clasped his arms about her. She stooped over him.

Then came Gift, running to his mother's side, and she put her hand on his head. There was something very beautiful about the young woman bending gracefully to touch the children: it moved many hearts.

'You have come to me, and there is love for you!'

They climbed onto the stage, men, women and children, until Odinstoy vanished in the knot of people.

'Oh my Gods,' Leander Fitzpatrick said, to his bonder-cameraman. 'Aren't you glad we came?'

'Byeee!'

Affie said, 'Have you seen about Odinstoy?' and the computer obediently spelled it out across the screen. She'd checked through her e-mails, and none were from Jason, so she was writing to him. What she wanted to say was: Why haven't you mailed me? What's going on? Have you spoken to your family yet? When will I be seeing the place at Olympus? When will we be married? But she couldn't say any of that, so she had to make do with talking about Odinstoy. Well, everyone else was.

Jason had to have seen something about her. Leander's report had been repeated and repeated, on the main Mars TV broadcast, on minor vid channels, on radio. Little clips of it had run on the front page of the newspaper, and on adverts for the newspaper. Leander said he'd even sold his report to Earth.

'Thank you both, darlings,' he'd mailed them. 'You've brought me luck. Send me an invite to the wedding! There is love for you!'

Affie couldn't make up her mind what she thought about it all. Of course, it was wonderful that Odinstoy

161

was having such success and becoming famous. It made Affie famous, in a way; and it was never going to hurt, to know someone like that.

But if the video was being shown on Earth . . . That was a little frightening. 'Odin is with us,' Odinstoy said.

'Odin's with *you*,' Affie wanted to say. 'What about me?' In fact, she wanted to say, 'What about me?' a lot. People's mouths dropped open when they saw Odinstoy, and their eyes lit up when they heard her name, and Affie wanted to say, 'What about *me*? I'm here too, and I'm *beautiful*!' But not even Jason had bothered to mail her.

It made her feel panicky and slightly sick. Back on Earth, when her father had shot himself, and she'd been told that she'd been bonded, when she'd felt scared and desperate, she'd mailed people for help. No one had answered, not even her mother.

This silence from Jason brought back that feeling of falling into a great pit with no help . . . She wasn't in such a desperate situation, of course . . . Well, not at first glance. She was on Mars, seventy-eight million kilometres from home, trying to make a new life . . . And Jason had promised her a new life, a life wonderfully like her old life on Earth, the lovely one she'd had before her father died. Comfortable, carefree, full of amusement and variety, safe. She wanted that *so much* . . .

She sent her mail. If there was no answer to this one, she would have to go back to Ares, and knock on the door of his flat. It would be embarrassing, but if a little embarrassment would get her what she wanted . . .

She left the mail-site and clicked to the news. There was a report about crop-yields – the people on Mars seemed obsessed with crop-yields – but that ended, and in its place came the increasingly familiar shot of Odinstoy, half-lit and naked, proclaiming, 'There is love for you!'

Affie cringed a little. What Odinstoy was doing was fabulous, of course; it was just what she wanted her to do, getting famous and all – but why did she have to take off every stitch in front of everybody? Grandads, and children, and even bonders. It was *so* . . .

She'd tried to say this to Toy, but Toy had looked at her with contempt and said, 'What would Mother Mars wear? A nice skirt and blouse?'

'No, but – You could have had a bit of drapery. Something wispy. Grecian—'

'Odin's Queen is *Grecian*?'

'Well, no, but – you didn't have to show everything to everybody!'

'I have nothing to hide,' Odinstoy said. 'When I speak for Odin, and Her, I'm telling the truth. Naked.'

Well, Affie thought, the truth was that Odinstoy was only a bonder really. So unsubtle.

The words of the report came through to her. '. . . For most of the sol, people have been gathered round the community hall, here in Osbourne.' And there they were, behind the reporter, holding glow-balls like the one Odinstoy had held on the stage. They could be heard chanting 'There is love for you' and 'Mother Mars, come to us'. It did look quite a dense crowd in the shot, but

Affie knew how deceptive such things could be. You could make ten people look like a huge crowd if you got them to stand together in a small space. 'It's not known where Odinstoy is,' said the reporter.

I know, Affie thought, smugly. She's in the shower room with Gift.

'Command. Screen off.' Affie stood up. If she walked over to the community hall, she could see these 'crowds' for herself. She got no further than the door of their small flat. The little screen beside the door showed her the view outside, and there were several people standing there.

'Command. Screen on.' She turned back to the computer. 'Command. Web-cam.' The computer screen showed a better picture. Five – no, six people, four women and two men, were standing and staring at the house. A couple of them held glow-balls. The manufacturers of those lamps, Affie thought, must be feeling grateful to Odinstoy too.

Affie was torn between a desire to go out and meet them – 'Yes, I'm Odinstoy's wife,' – and a desire to hide from them.

'Oh, you're Odinstoy's *wife*,' they'd say. 'Oh, it must be wonderful to be her wife. What's she like, what's she really like?' Affie was getting sick of it.

Jason *had* to answer her. If he didn't, she really was going into Ares to find him.

Then she'd be Jason's wife.

She shook off that thought. She'd be Jason's rich, amazingly beautiful, incredibly well-dressed and charming, talented wife. Everyone would say, 'How did he deserve *her*? What a lucky man.' Nobody said Odinstoy was lucky to have her. They all thought *she* was lucky to be with Odinstoy. And if she left Odinstoy for Jason, she'd be rid of Gift. There was a happy thought.

The reporter was moving among the people, some clutching glow-balls, and asking them what they thought of Odinstoy. 'She's fantastic,' they said; and, 'She's wonderful, I can't believe it!'

'She's just so great!'

'She's, like, total! Totally total!'

If they'd all been like that, Zeuslove would have worried less, but there were others. A solemn, bearded man said, 'The God was there. I felt Him. He brought the Goddess to us – not a Goddess imported from Earth, but Mars's own, true Goddess. This is an important day.'

A woman with grey, curly hair looked into the camera and said, 'My life has changed.'

People who squealed, 'She's total!', Zeuslove thought, would have forgotten Odinstoy in a couple of weeks. People who solemnly said, 'My life has changed,' and 'This is an important day,' didn't forget anywhere near so soon, if they ever did.

Adonai Cooper, a priest of Apollo from Paris, one of Ares's outlying suburbs, uncrossed and recrossed his legs. 'She's preaching that all bonders should be freed.'

Zeuslove nodded. He knew.

'Relax,' Jason said. 'Nobody's going to free their

bonders.' He was sitting on the other side of Zeuslove's desk, leaning back in his chair, one ankle resting on his other knee.

Zeuslove, his eyes still on the computer screen, merely smiled. Adonai said sharply, 'You'll no doubt be delighted when your bonders begin instructing you on how to run your household, and demanding payment!'

Zeuslove looked up. 'Do you own a house, Jason – or any bonders?'

Jason smirked at Adonai. 'Not any more.'

'Jason's father tired of paying his bills and buying him out of trouble.'

'He's an old fussbudget, always was,' Jason said, grinning at Adonai. 'Just because I got a few bonders pregnant!'

'Other men's bonders,' Zeuslove said.

Jason laughed. 'They were getting another bonder for nothing!'

'Don't hide your talents,' Zeuslove said. 'There was the bonder you killed with an overdose, and the Freechild girl you maimed.'

'Maimed!' Adonai said.

'Don't get excited,' Jason said. 'It was only an accident. Car crash.'

'You turned the computer off?' Adonai said.

Jason laughed. 'Where's the fun if you don't?'

Adonai grimaced, as if at a stink, and looked at Zeuslove.

'Jason has been working for me,' Zeuslove said, as if in explanation.

Adonai looked puzzled, and as if the stink under his nose had worsened.

'It's been such hard labour,' Jason said. 'Living in a beautiful apartment, going to parties, sexing a beautiful girl – I'm worn out.'

'And?' Zeuslove said.

'Oh, I'm worth three times what you're paying me. They're not married, never were.'

'Who're not?' Adonai asked.

'Odinstoy and Affroditey Atkinson,' Zeuslove said. 'Also known as Freya Atkinson.'

'Atkinson's not their name,' Jason said. 'Odinstoy doesn't have a name – she's a freed bonder—'

'We all know that,' Adonai said.

'Then here's something you *don't* know: Affie's real name is Millington. She comes from a wealthy Earth family, but her father got into debt and started borrowing money from everywhere and everybody. Borrowed money against his darling daughter. Got in deeper and deeper, and then shot himself. Debts are called in and Affie finds herself a bonder overnight. The silly mare didn't know what had hit her. But here's the good stuff – she was bought by the parents of the little boy; you know, Odinstoy's photogenic little boy.'

Understanding came to the faces of the other two men.

'When Odinstoy got the chance to come here, as God-speaker for Odin, she had Affie kidnap the little boy – and, by the way, Affie is *still* a bonder. She has a false ID.'

167

'Abduction and theft,' Zeuslove said, closing his eyes as he nodded.

'Am I good or what?' Jason asked. 'How many people could have got all that out of her in a couple of days? I think I should get a bonus.' He was hoping to impress Zeuslove. In truth, it had been easier than he'd ever imagined. Affie was a fool, who'd fall into bed and confide in any one who said to her, 'I love you'.

'I'll consider it,' Zeuslove said.

'When?' Jason asked.

'When I've verified your account. Until then, consider your payment to be the time spent in my apartment, spending my money.' He held up a hand to check whatever it was Jason was about to say. 'You're dismissed.'

Sitting sharply forward in his chair, Jason said, 'I think—'

'Dismissed!'

Jason thought about arguing, but Zeuslove would only call security. He jumped out of his chair and swung out of the office, not bothering to hide his anger. As he reached the lifts, his phone bleeped. Raising his wrist, he looked at the screen on his watch, and saw that yet another message had come through from Affie.

He didn't need to read it. Whatever it said, the message was the same: When am I going to see you again? When are you going to marry me? She'd actually believed all that!

She was very beautiful, very beautiful indeed – and she wasn't likely to be on Mars much longer – so why not see her again, sex her a few more times?

But a great irritation seized him. She might be beautiful, but she wasn't good company – just a silly little girl. No good in bed either – just kissy, kissy, cuddly, cooey girly stuff. True, he had no need to play along with that any more, but—

He just couldn't be bothered. It might be fun to show her what a good time *really* was – make the lights in her hair turn white – but then he'd have all the weeping and wailing to put up with, and if his fun spoiled Zeuslove's plans, whatever they were, then there'd be Hades and the Furies to pay.

Zeuslove had his information, so there was no need to keep playing the game. He sent a message back. 'Affie, sweetheart. Stop calling me, stop texting me. I'm not going to take you to Olympus, and my family would kick you out of the house – you cheap little ex-bonder immigrant, you. And marry you? I'd only marry you if I was paid, and you don't have any money. So stop wasting my time. Byeee!'

TV Mars

The broadcast was from New Oldbury, another of Mars's Aesir settlements; and there was a shot of Odinstoy, arms raised, crying, 'There is love, there is love, there is love!' Her arms and shoulders were naked, but the camera discreetly panned no lower, and hid the fact that the rest of her was naked too.

Cut to a bearded man, who said, 'We're grateful that Odinstoy could come to us.' From behind him came chanting. Glancing back for a moment, he smiled slightly. 'We were very keen to see her for ourselves. It has been a wonderful day.'

The camera cut to a young woman. 'What did you think of Odinstoy?' asked the unseen interviewer.

'Oh, she was total, just total.' She put her hand to her heart and searched for words. 'Oh just fabby total.'

'I feel privileged to have been there,' said a young man.

A group of young men stood before the camera, arms round each other's shoulders. They waved clenched fists as they chanted, 'Mother Mars! Mother Mars! Mars Mars Mars!'

*

News-sheets in hundreds of homes flickered as they picked up the latest transmissions to their pages: '*Whatever you think of the incomer, Odinstoy, and her revelation of "Mother Mars", it must lead us to ask ourselves, Why do we worship Mother Earth? Why do we permit Earth to dictate, through the Church of Mars, who will get the best-paid, most secure jobs? Why do we despise our own productions and run after the fashions, the culture of Earth? Why are we, still, in so many ways, in thrall to the Blue Planet? Aren't we mature enough, even now, to stand on our own feet?*'

'We've had so many requests!' Rebecca said. 'She can't possibly do them all. And it's getting to be more than I can cope with, so—'

'There's not that many gatherings,' someone said. 'You're exaggerating if you're saying she couldn't visit them all.'

Rebecca picked up some of the print-outs she had in front of her and waved them. 'Gatherings for Odin, for Thor, for The Twins . . . there's even a mail here – somewhere – from a temple of Dionysus—'

There were exclamations of surprise around the table, and some laughter.

'What do the Greeks want with a God-speaker for Odin?'

'It's Mother Mars,' Rebecca said, 'not Odin, that they're interested in.'

'Oh.'

'That explains it.'

'But it's not just gatherings,' Rebecca said. 'There's a store here, in Chiltern, that wants her to open their – what? – their "refurbished children's department" . . . And the University of Ares wants her to give a talk, and there's people wanting interviews, and people who want a lock of her hair, or for her to bless something and send it to them—'

'Like what?'

'They say, "some small object". All these have to be read, and answered – or *thought* about, at least. And I have enough to do with organising the Wedding. Can someone else take this on?'

No one was listening. All round the table, people were leaning forward, eyes brightening.

'The Wedding! How is that coming along?'

'Has anything been decided?'

Rebecca sighed. 'Odinstoy says it's to happen next year, in May.'

'May!' someone said. 'We're in thrall to the Blue Planet, right enough!'

There was laughter around the table. A year on Mars was a little more than twice the length of an Earth year; and while the single Earth moon waxed and waned with each Earth month, there were two moons rising and setting around Mars. And yet the names of the Earth months had been kept on Mars, though they had little meaning.

'What's the *point*?' someone said. 'It's just a waste of money!'

'Odin is going to marry Mother Mars!' Thorsgift said, as if the point of that was self-evident.

'It's Odin's favour,' Rebecca said. 'It's a sign that Odin approves of what we're doing here on Mars—'

'That we are *Mars*!' said a young woman, banging her fist on the table. 'And not just a second-rate Earth!'

'Well, I'm not sure—' Rebecca said.

'I am!' said the young woman. 'It's saying, Wake up, Mars!'

'Come to Mother!' said a man, and everyone laughed.

'But you know what I mean,' the young woman said.

'What I was trying to say,' Rebecca went on, 'is that, if everyone wants this ceremony – as they seem to do – then I have more than enough on my plate in trying to sort that out. I can't answer all these mails and texts as well. Someone else must take them on.'

Looks were exchanged around the table. Excuses were mumbled. Then Thorsgift said, 'Why not Affie?'

Rebecca looked up. 'Affie?'

'Why not?'

'Well—' said the young woman, and laughed.

'Is she going to cope?' Rebecca asked.

'Let her try,' Thorsgift said. 'It'll give her something to do. She's been a bit down lately.'

Affie sat in front of the computer, feeling that her whole body was made of lead – heavy and ugly and base. Answer these e-mails, she'd been told. God-speakers' wives usually act as secretaries for their spouse.

She supposed that she'd better answer at least *some* of them, or it would be nag, nag, nag . . .

No, be sensible, some small, sensible part of herself told her. You're here on Mars now. There's no way back. You have to make a new life here, the best life you can. Here's a way to do it . . .

Because her new life wasn't going to be as Jason's wife.

She was leaden again. She didn't even want to cry. She just wanted to sit there, a lump of misery, staring at nothing, doing nothing . . . Because she was nothing.

She wasn't sorry about losing Jason – not that she had lost him, when she'd never had him. Now she had no hope of his money or his homes, it was quite easy to remember him clearly and say that she'd never liked him. She'd even thought him quite ugly.

Oh Gods, she thought. All Gods, any Gods – am I really that shallow? It was like catching sight of herself in a mirror when she looked at her very worst: lank, greasy hair, puffy, tired eyes . . .

Maybe she *was* shallow, but fear was what had made her grab at Jason.

Now the fear was saying: Better make yourself useful, or Odinstoy will be chucking you too.

So, answer some e-mails.

But she was too leaden. Instead, she sighed heavily, and, bored with the computer screen, looked vaguely around the room.

It was a beautiful room. The Taylors knew how to live. They were probably Osbourne's wealthiest family, with a private dome on the edge of the village, and much land surrounding it. They were members of the Osbourne gathering, and knew that life was becoming fraught for Odinstoy, because her followers crowded into Osbourne every day. They stood outside the community hall, holding their glow-balls, and they stood outside Odinstoy's house. Gift had begun to be frightened by the crowds who pushed and shoved around him whenever he appeared, wanting locks of his hair and buttons from his clothing. Wulfstan Taylor had phoned through on the computer, offering his farmhouse as a refuge.

Even Odinstoy had been glad to accept. When they'd left their flat, the crowd had penned them in, all wanting to speak to Odinstoy and to touch her. She did say something to all of them, so it took a long time to travel a couple of metres, and even then the crowd followed them. When they boarded the mono, Odinstoy had to ask them, as a special favour, not to get on with them.

When they arrived at the Taylors' dome, the whole Taylor family, and some interested friends, had been waiting to greet them. Wulfstan Taylor, a big, brown man with white hair, had shaken Odinstoy by the hand, saying, 'You're welcome. We're honoured to welcome Odin's Voice, and you're all welcome, but –' he'd grinned '– don't ask me to free my bonders!'

Odinstoy had smiled back. 'You don't believe I speak for Odin, then?'

Still smiling, Taylor had said, 'I think Odin doesn't have to make this farm pay! And what about my old Arris?

Seventy, if he's a day, and what would he do if I freed him? Ask Odin that! But I must introduce you to my wife—'

Freewoman Taylor had taken Odinstoy's hand in both of hers, and said, 'You're very, very welcome, and you must ask for anything you need. Please do.'

'And my sons –' said Wulfstan, introducing two teenage boys. Affie noted that the oldest was only about fourteen, and so of little interest to her.

'And my daughter –' A little girl of about nine, who stared at them both in astonishment.

'Our bonders talk of nothing but you!' Freewoman Taylor had said. 'It's so funny!'

Odinstoy had bared her teeth in a smile.

'One of mine,' a guest had said, 'begged my news-paper – did you see that piece they did on you, God-speaker? I expect you did. It was because of that. I said, "Well, what's the use, because as soon as the next news is broadcast, that piece'll be gone." She said, "Oh no, I'll freeze it so it doesn't pick up any more, and I'll keep it!" So I let her have it – but *I'd* forgotten that you could freeze news-sheets like that! It comes to something when bonders know more than we do!'

'Oh, I leave most things to my Patsy,' another guest had said. 'She's far more capable than I am. It's my children who never stop talking about you, Odinstoy. I'm sure I hear your name, and "Mother Mars" five hundred times a day!'

Odinstoy's face had become expressionless. 'Odin says—' she'd begun, but Affie had broken in:

'What a fabulous place! I can't wait to see inside! I bet it's *beyond*!'

Odinstoy had smiled and fallen silent, perhaps acknowledging that this wasn't the time to start an argument. They'd been standing outside the house, though still under the dome. Around them were lawns and flowerbeds. A stream ran past, edged with reeds and water-flowers, and there was even an oak tree, sheltering a small family shrine to Thor.

Most of the house seemed to be glass. 'We don't get as much sunlight as you do on Earth,' Taylor had said. 'We let in as much as we can.'

'Why have roofs at all?' Affie had asked, wondering if she could be a rich and famous architect.

'You'd get very wet, sweetheart, when the irrigation systems switch on,' Taylor had said.

They'd given Affie a whole big room to herself – bigger than the whole of their flat in Osbourne. It had an en-suite too, with real water – though the en-suite was shared by the room occupied by Odinstoy and Gift, which was a pity. A bath, though, and real water!

Her room was big enough for chairs and a table, a computer screen, and a whole wall of clothes cupboards. And everything – the bright rug, the bedclothes, the curtains – was of the best quality, as good as anything on Earth.

The whole house was like it: the Taylors were wealthy people, and kept several bonders. The house and garden was enclosed safely in its own dome, served by its own mono-link; while the dome was surrounded by the fields and woods that had created the wealth to build it.

Jason's place at Olympia must be similar, but even bigger, and with a lake and a beach. And a boat. But Jason had called her 'a cheap little ex-bonder immigrant'. Odinstoy had been right. That was another thing that hurt. Odinstoy was only a bonder – a bonder born and bred, even if she was free now, but she'd been *right*. She hadn't even met Jason, and yet she'd been right about him straight away . . .

But probably, she'd only said what she'd said about Jason because she was jealous, and it was just by coincidence that she'd turned out to be right.

Honestly, said one half of Affie to the other half, you are a shit, Affie Millington. Why should Odinstoy be jealous of *Jason*? She's got most of Mars running after her at the moment.

And who got you away from being the Perrys' bonder? Who brought you to Mars? Who got you this lovely room in the Taylors' lovely house? Odinstoy, that's who. The Taylors would never have invited you by yourself. All right, Odinstoy might have shoved you and slapped you a couple of times, and she *is* a bonder, but she's helped you more than anybody else has ever done.

You'd better start helping her, said Affie's sensible side; or you're going to be all on your own. On Mars.

And a little gratitude might not hurt. Even if she is a bonder.

So stop moping! Do something! Be useful! Show some gratitude!

Answer three mails for Odinstoy, she bargained with herself, and then you can – oh, look at some fashion sites.

The first e-mail was asking for a lock of Odinstoy's hair. Odinstoy had already sorted this. 'I'm not cutting lumps out of my hair,' she'd said. 'Get bits of blessed cloth. Send everybody who asks for hair a bit of cloth, and explain.'

Affie, now she came to think of it, had the little squares of cloth in a box, close to hand. They were the remains of an old pillowcase, donated by Freewoman Taylor. John had cut them up, and Odinstoy really had kissed and blessed each one, in the names of Odin and Mother Mars.

Affie put an envelope in the printer, copied the address from the e-mail, and printed it. Then she dictated a few words to the computer: 'Thank you for your communication. I enclose a square of blessed cloth . . .' She signed off with, 'Blessings from Odin and Mother Mars.'

She put the letter and cloth in the envelope, sealed it, and set it aside.

One done! She felt a little less leaden, a little more cheerful.

So, next one! An 'informal discussion group' in Chesney – a district of Ares – would like Odinstoy to come and talk to them. Scrawled in one corner of the letter were the notes Affie had taken when she'd read the mail to Odinstoy. The answer was yes – they'd both agreed that Odinstoy should talk to as many people as she could. The discussion group had suggested dates, and Affie called up Odinstoy's diary, to check that she wouldn't be double-booking her. She then chose a date that she felt would be convenient, and mailed the group back. She asked the group to pay Odinstoy's expenses and said that, although Odinstoy charged no fee, it would be hugely helpful if they made a donation towards 'Odinstoy's work'. This last was entirely Affie's idea, and she was very pleased with it. If you wanted to be rich as well as famous, the money had to come from somewhere.

She sent the mail off and looked round for the next. She was enjoying herself. When she'd first been sent all the mails and letters, and more or less told to deal with them, she'd first felt insulted – it seemed such a mundane, demeaning task – and then she'd felt rather overwhelmed. She'd never done anything like it. Where was she to begin?

But now she was started, she found she enjoyed it. Making these decisions, deciding when and where Odinstoy would speak, filling in the diary – it made her feel efficient, high-powered, intelligent. She got such a buzz from it that she answered five mails, one after another, and then she felt light enough to rise from her chair and walk to the window.

Below, on the lawn, Odinstoy sat a table, with an interviewer from a blog. Affie had arranged the date and time for the interview, and had persuaded Odinstoy to meet the reporter; and seeing them gave Affie a feeling of satisfaction. It seemed to be going well too, as far as she could tell without being able to hear. Odinstoy was leaning forward, gesturing, talking, no doubt being charming and annoying. The reporter was leaning forward too, apparently intent. I am doing a good job, Affie thought. The feeling was a novelty.

Odinstoy was wearing a lovely suit, in a shimmering, silvery material, of wide-legged trousers and a fitted jacket. It had been given to her, for nothing, by – oh, either by the Ares store that stocked them, or by the person who'd made it. Affie couldn't remember just at the moment. Odinstoy had been given so many things: a bottle of 'War God' vodka, a watch, children's clothes, toys, jewellery . . . They were all attempts, it seemed, to get Odinstoy's attention, so she would 'work with' that person or company and not another. Affie accepted all gifts, with thanks, and invited the company to suggest how Odinstoy might work with them.

It seemed that Odinstoy was becoming famous – *was* famous. Fame and riches always went together, didn't they? Riches would come. Odinstoy would, one day, have a big house like the Taylors'; she'd have her own car, fancy clothes, a wonderful apartment in town like Jason's, and another out at Olympus or somewhere even better . . . And if I'm still with Odinstoy, Affie thought, if I'm her business partner and manager – well, then, I can laugh at Jason.

A beep from the computer called her back. A mail had come in. Feeling strong and efficient again, Affie sat down to answer it, expecting it to be another request for a blessing from Odinstoy.

Instead it said, 'Please allow me to introduce myself. My name is Alvin Pope, and I produce *Mars Here and Now* for Channel 50. My brief is to cover topical news and promote discussion, so naturally I'm very keen to feature Odinstoy on the programme, as she is so much in the news "here and now". I would love it if I could interview Odinstoy, hear a little about her life, hear more about Mother Mars. In the second half of the programme, if we could, I'd like to chair a discussion between Odinstoy and some of the people from the other side of the debate. I already have an agreement from Zeuslove Thatcher, whom you may know of (in case you don't, he's the Archpriest of Zeus). I'd be delighted if Odinstoy would agree. Hoping to hear from you soon, yours sincerely, Alvin Pope.'

Affie read this through several times, and decided that Odinstoy had to agree. This was just what they needed. She was tempted to send back a reply saying yes before she'd even discussed it with Toy.

Instead, after some thought, she sent back a reply saying that she would get back to him as soon as she'd talked the offer over with Odinstoy, but in the meantime, what was the appearance fee? She signed it 'A. Atkinson, secretary,' and felt that glow of efficiency again.

The Interview

The Taylors' eldest son, Barley, volunteered to be Odinstoy's guide to the studio, 'to make sure she doesn't get lost'.

'But they can take a taxi!' his mother said.

'I'll help them with the taxis,' Barley said. 'I'll make sure they get there on time.'

Freewoman Taylor pulled a face at Odinstoy and Affie, to apologise for her son's insistence on going along with them.

Odinstoy reached out and put her hand on Barley's shoulder. 'I am glad to have his help.'

Barley stood taller, smiled, and sent his mother a quenching look.

'Little Gift and – ah – John – can stay here,' Freewoman Taylor said. 'We'll take good care of them. I'm sure they'd be bored at the studio!'

Odinstoy smiled and slightly ducked her head in thanks, but said, 'They will come with me.'

'At least leave the bonder-boy!' Freewoman Taylor said.

John looked as if he'd been slapped. His face reddened,

and he stood to one side of their group, as if wondering whether he should join them.

Odinstoy said, 'Why would I leave behind my other son?' John beamed, and went instantly to her side – while Freewoman Taylor looked as if she'd been slapped.

They'd travelled by the family's mono-link to the mainline, where a surprising number of people were waiting, sitting on the platform and leaning against the walls. When they saw Odinstoy, a gabble rose from them, and they flocked in from all directions to surround her.

'Odinstoy! Odinstoy!'

'I was there – I saw you – in Osbourne!'

'I saw it on the web – I've watched it over and over!'

'Odinstoy – over here!'

Affie, despite her beauty, found herself pushed aside, and jostled to and fro by people who didn't see her, even as they were shoving her out of the way. It was frightening – not only the physical manhandling, which bruised her dignity and made her fear being knocked down and trampled, but the sense of having become invisible.

Odinstoy was talking and smiling, holding Gift in front of her and John against her side. Affie glimpsed them occasionally through gaps in the crowd. The mono they had meant to catch slid to a halt beside them, and then left without them.

Barley surfaced at Affie's side. 'We're going to be late!' he said, and pushed and shoved towards Odinstoy.

They wriggled, pushed, persuaded and struggled their way to the edge of the platform, and got on the next mono, but many of Odinstoy's followers got on with them. Throughout the journey to Ares, they chanted, 'Mother Mars! Mother Mars!' The other passengers either stared and frowned, or pretended they hadn't noticed anything. Affie was mortified.

The followers were useful once they arrived in Ares. Several of them had a much better idea of how to find the nearest taxi-point than Barley. 'If you ever need to go anywhere,' one of them told Affie, as they walked, 'just come to us and we'll get you there. Or if you need anything. Anything. There's nothing we wouldn't do for *her*.'

Strange people, Affie thought. Odinstoy had been born a bonder, and she'd been made into one and forced to serve, to fetch and carry. But these people – free people by the look of them – *wanted* to serve.

Affie, Odinstoy, Gift and John all got into the same taxi, and Barley climbed in after them. 'Get your own!' he said rudely, to one of the followers who wanted to get in after them.

'There's room!' the girl said.

'No, there's not!' Barley said, and pressed the button to close the doors. It was true that there wasn't really room, with all of them inside, but it was so obvious that Barley wanted to be their only help and guide that Affie couldn't help smiling.

She looked back through the rear window and saw that the followers were piling into the taxis that were left – and more taxis were arriving, signalled by the demand for the first few.

The studio, when they reached it, was disappointing. Affie had expected it to be a glamorous, beautiful place, but it was a shed, built among other sheds. The other taxis drew up as they were getting out of their own, and the crowd followed them right to the door, and seemed ready to follow them inside, until Odinstoy turned and told them to wait. 'I have to go now and tell everyone about Mother Mars.'

There was a clamour. 'But Odinstoy—'

'We can—'

'We'll—'

She didn't try to speak, simply held up her hand, her face blank. To Affie's surprise, the little crowd of followers fell quiet. 'I want you to stay here,' Odinstoy said.

The crowd fell back, and let them get near the doors. 'We'll wait for you!' someone called, and there was cheering and more chants of 'Mother Mars'.

Affie went with Odinstoy into the building, as of right, feeling proud that everyone could see that she had a special place at Odinstoy's side, and also very glad to be getting away from the mad people. She was already wondering whether, when the interview was over, they could creep out the back way and avoid them. Just inside the doors, they all realised at once that Barley wasn't with them, and turned to wait for him. He was outside the doors, and waved to them, signalling, 'I'm going to stay here'.

Fancy wanting to stay with those strange people, Affie thought.

The studio's reception area was, frankly, scruffy. There

was a small desk with a person who was probably a bonder sitting behind it; but much of the other space was taken up with boxes and parcels piled in untidy heaps. Affie stepped up to the desk, dodging in front of Odinstoy, and said, 'This is *Odinstoy*.' The man looked at Odinstoy and, judging by his expression, he'd heard of her. Affie felt gratified. 'She's here to meet Alvin Pope.'

'Take a seat. I'll let Freeman Pope know.'

They found some seats among the box piles and sat down. Alvin Pope, a thin, keen young man, came down to meet them within a few minutes, and seemed a little startled by the many faces peering through the glass doors, as Odinstoy's followers kept an eye on her. He also wasn't very happy to see the children, though he said nothing, and thought he was keeping it to himself. They exchanged greetings and shook hands, and Pope led them to a lift. 'We're so glad you agreed to do this,' Pope said, as they rose through the floors. 'It'll just be a brief chat about your life and achievements, nothing to worry about – and then we'll bring on Archpriest Thatcher. You don't mind exchanging views with him, I hope?'

Odinstoy said nothing, so it was left to Affie to say, 'We agreed to it. Of course we don't mind.'

'Good. You're a little late. We'll have to crack on, I'm afraid. I was hoping to have time to chat, but . . . Er – perhaps we could have the boys taken to the café round the corner?'

'I'll look after Gift,' John said. 'I'll keep him quiet.'

Pope looked from Odinstoy to Affie. 'He will,' Odinstoy said.

'O-K,' Pope said, doubtfully. 'I'll take you straight to the studio.'

They followed him through narrow corridors with glass walls, which looked out on the dome and its maintenance bridges. Inside, though, were torn carpets and faded, dated décor.

Pope stopped. 'Would it be possible to leave the children here? They'd be a little in the way – we weren't expecting—'

John, holding Gift's hand, looked up at Odinstoy. She crouched down and kissed them both. Stroking back John's hair, she said, 'Stay close.'

Pope led them on into a covered, dark stretch of corridor, where there were doors on both sides, and then through a thick, padded door into a tiny room all but filled by a low table holding flickering news-sheets, and three big chairs. A man was sitting in one of the chairs. As soon as they came in, he sprang up, and shouted, 'Hello there! Sol!'

Affie put her hand to her nose and whispered to Odinstoy, 'That's Diomedes Faringdon.' She knew because, unlike Odinstoy, she was able to read the news and blogs that were broadcast to news-sheets. Faringdon, she knew, was quite famous on Mars.

'So pleased to meet you at last, Odinstoy,' Faringdon said, seizing rather than taking her hand. 'Do I call you Odinstoy? Take a seat. I'll just run through—'

'We'd better go to the control room,' Pope said to Affie, and she had to leave Odinstoy alone with the rather fierce, if cheerful, Faringdon. She hoped Odinstoy could cope.

The control room was next door. It was also small and crowded, with a big window that showed them Odinstoy and Faringdon crammed into the studio. There were several small screens, too, showing how it looked to viewers. On the screens, the studio Odinstoy and Faringdon were in appeared to be a large and comfortable room. 'You can sit here and watch,' Pope said, showing her an unoccupied chair at the back, well away from the control desk. 'Don't worry; you won't be in the way.'

Affie, who hadn't been worried, sat and watched him take his place at the desk in front of the studio window. She glanced round at the other people, who were listening on headphones, studying the screen, or operating switches, all appearing very busy – and then saw, with a start, that Zeuslove Thatcher was sitting opposite her, rubbing his chin with his fingers as he watched. She recognised him from news-sheets and broadcasts, but it was a shock to see him a metre away. You didn't expect to see an Archpriest in a suit and outside a temple, without a ritual knife in his hand. It was unnatural, somehow.

'Quiet, everybody,' Pope said. 'Ssh. Bags of hush. OK, Di.'

'Well, good evening everyone,' Diomedes Faringdon said. 'With us this evening we have a young woman who's been very much in the news recently – Odinstoy. Good evening, Odinstoy.'

Odinstoy didn't answer, and for a moment Affie felt panic. What was the matter? Stage-fright? Then Odinstoy said quite calmly, 'Good evening.'

'Now, I don't think we should bore everyone with the usual biography,' Faringdon said. '*Everyone* knows you were born on Earth, *everyone* knows you were born a bonder – though, come to think of it, what was that *like*?'

Silence. 'What was what like?'

'Being a bonder.'

Silence. Then, 'It was like,' Odinstoy said, 'being a bonder.'

'Yes,' Faringdon said keenly, 'but could you give us some *insight*?'

After another silence, Odinstoy said, 'Ask your own bonders.'

Faringdon shuffled some papers. 'I must be sure to do that. You were still actually a bonder when you first spoke for Odin. How did that happen?'

'Odin spoke to me.'

'And what was *that* like?'

'Odin speaks to you too. All the time. If you can't hear Him, I can't help you.'

Faringdon laughed. 'I can see this isn't going to be one of my easier interviews. But tell me – you were freed, in fact, because of your gift for hearing Odin. How did that come about?'

'Because Odin wished it. He wanted me to be freed, so I could come to Mars and tell everyone here about Mother Mars.'

'Ah, yes, Mother Mars,' Faringdon said. 'I think we have a clip . . .'

In the control room, they were poised to play the clip. It was, of course, the clip of Odinstoy, naked, proclaiming that 'there is love for you!' Everyone must have seen it a hundred times, but Affie noticed Archpriest Thatcher watching it, his face calm and thoughtful. In the studio, Odinstoy and Faringdon sat, waiting, until the clip ended.

'It seems there was a ready audience for the revelation of Mother Mars,' Faringdon said, when the interview resumed. Affie hoped that Odinstoy knew what he meant. 'In fact, I understand that you had to leave your house because of the nuisance of your fans constantly hanging about outside . . .' He left space for Odinstoy to say something, but she was silent. 'In fact, there are fans outside the studio at this moment. Can we . . . ?'

The picture on the screen changed to one of the people outside. Affie recognised some who had sat near them on the mono and walked beside them on their way to the taxi-point.

'They're chanting, "Mother Mars, Mother Mars",' Faringdon said. 'They can keep it up for hours!' The picture on the screen changed to the studio shot again. 'I believe they call themselves, "Odinstoy's Bonders". Did you expect this sort of reaction?'

'They serve the God, not me. They're Odin's bonders. We all are.'

'Odinstoy – thank you.' Faringdon turned to face the camera. 'Of course, not everyone has been so bowled over by Mother Mars's charms. Some people have been severely critical . . .'

Affie was distracted by Archpriest Thatcher rising from his seat and leaving the control room.

'I'd like to bring in, if I may, the Archpriest of Zeus, Archpriest Thatcher –'

A figure appeared on the screen – Archpriest Thatcher, in his neat suit, with his neat beard. It was a strange effect, to see a man leave the room, large as life, and then appear, shrunken, on the little screen. But if she shifted her eyes a little, she could look through the window into the studio, and there was Archpriest Thatcher, life-size again, taking his seat.

'– who has spoken out most strongly against Odinstoy, and especially against her revelation of Mother Mars. Welcome, Archpriest. I'm grateful that you've found time to appear with us here today. Can I ask you, first of all, why the revelation of Mother Mars concerns you so much?'

Archpriest Thatcher hitched himself a little higher in his seat. 'It's corrupting. And distracting. Mars is still, even now, Diomedes, a young society. We have many problems to face, and we need to be strong, united. We need our young people to be brought up with the same, clear values, so they can work together, know right from wrong, and keep on the right road. This talk of "Mother Mars" – it divides us, it weakens us.'

('Camera on Odinstoy, please, on Odinstoy.')

'Surely,' Faringdon said, almost sounding as if he was

going to laugh, 'we would all be just as united, us Martians, as children of Mother Mars? Perhaps even more so.'

'From what I understand, Diomedes, this "Mother Mars" is a Fertility Goddess, a Mother Goddess – in which case, she is simply an aspect of Demeter, or, indeed, of several existing Goddesses. There are already temples to Demeter. We don't need any new, invented "Mother Mars".'

'But Demeter is an Earth Goddess, whose concern is the fertility of Earth! Don't we deserve our own Goddess? That's what people are saying.'

'It's what the misguided and confused are saying, certainly. And there lies the danger. There are always misguided and confused people in any society; and all of us can become misguided and confused at any time. Then we need to be helped out of that state – not to be seduced by people who wish to exploit us, and confuse us further, leading us still further astray.'

'Strong words,' Faringdon said.

'The truth. Moreover, her preaching that bonders should be freed is purely mischievous. I don't hear the voice of any God in it. I hear the voice of a bonder, misguided and confused who, in a spirit of anger and petty spite, wishes to destroy our way of life and our economy.'

Faringdon swung round to face his other guest. 'Odinstoy: you're accused of being misguided, confused, angry, pettily spiteful, and of wishing to seduce and exploit us poor Martians – oh, and also of wishing to destroy our way of life and economy. Anything to say?'

Odinstoy was leaning her head on her hand, her face impassive. She said, 'I spoke for Odin.'

'Yes, but to the accusations that—?'

'Everything I said, I said for Odin.'

'Who is simply an aspect of Hermes,' said the Archpriest, and the camera snapped back to him. 'And, since Hermes is the God of Liars, very fitting.'

'Dear me, you're now accused of lying,' Faringdon said to Odinstoy. 'Any comment?'

'I don't make the accusation lightly,' the Archpriest said. 'I happen to know that the woman who calls herself "Freya Atkinson", whom Odinstoy claims to be her wife and a Freewoman, is, in fact, neither.'

Affie felt as if she'd been shot through the heart, the shock was so sharp and unpleasant. And, even in the busy control room, she saw several people turn and gape at her before hastily remembering their jobs.

'I happen to know,' the Archpriest continued, 'that "Freya Atkinson" is, in truth, Affroditey Millington, a runaway bonder. She came to Mars with false ID, and the help of Odinstoy.' He couldn't repress a sneer. 'Odinstoy is a thief. She stole a bonder.'

How does he know? Affie's brain scrabbled through a thousand things – did his God tell him, as Odin spoke to Odinstoy? How did he know? If not his God, who had told him?

Diomedes Faringdon seemed taken aback, but was still enjoying himself. 'Good Gods! This is a serious accusation. I hope you've considered—'

'I know that what I say is the truth. Does Odinstoy deny it?'

The camera flashed to Odinstoy's face. She looked grim, but said nothing.

Affie's mind was still in turmoil. Who knew? she asked herself. Who could have told him? Only Odinstoy and I knew – Oh, and Thorsgift, but *he* wouldn't . . . And we haven't . . . And then she knew. She knew whom she'd told, and who was the only person who could have told the Archpriest.

'And does she deny this?' the Archpriest asked. 'That the child she calls her son is not her son at all?'

'Great Gods, Archpriest,' Faringdon said, amused. 'Then whose son is he? Mine?'

'He is the son of a couple on Earth, a Freeman and Freewoman Perry. His real name is Apollo Perry. The girl who now calls herself Odinstoy's wife was their bonder and looked after the child. Odinstoy persuaded the girl to abduct the child in return for helping her to run away from her owners.'

Affie, in the control room, got to her feet. She tried to speak, to say it wasn't true, but her voice had dried. Her eyes stung as tears filled them. Wasn't it enough, she thought, for Jason to lie to me and make a fool of me and shame me? Did he have to do this as well?

What exactly had Jason done? Sold what she'd told him to a newsblog, just because Odinstoy was in the news? But then, why hadn't they seen the story before the Archpriest spoke? Why was everyone in the control room so surprised?

A nasty little thought occurred to her. Jason had only befriended her – had only flattered her and fooled her – so he could find out these things. And then betray her. And she'd betrayed Odinstoy.

The camera was showing Odinstoy. 'Is there anything you'd like to say?' Faringdon asked.

'Gift *is* my child,' Odinstoy said. Her voice was unsteady. Affie, watching, could tell that she was very angry, and felt a sharp pain in her heart. There was nothing Odinstoy cared for as much as her child. She'd rescued Affie from bondery and Earth, in order to keep Gift. And now, because of Affie, she was going to lose him.

'Gift was in my belly,' Odinstoy said. 'The Perrys took him from me. They are the thieves. They stole my child. I only took him back.'

'And stole the Perrys' bonder while you were about it,' Faringdon said.

'Odin tells me there should be no bonders.'

The Archpriest spoke up again. 'Excuse me, Diomedes; there's been another untruth. Odinstoy was a bonder when she gave birth to the child; therefore the child is *not* hers. It belongs to her owners. Also, by her own admission, the father of the child was Freeman Perry, her owner. The child is therefore doubly his, and – this person – who preaches to us – is an abductor and a thief.'

'"By her own admission"?' Faringdon said. 'When did she admit it? I haven't heard her admit it.' He made a show of pressing keys on the laptop in front of him. 'My researchers haven't heard her admit it.'

'I have statements in my possession,' Zeuslove said, 'made by people who heard her admit it.'

'Oh? And when shall we be hearing from these people?'

'Why don't we hear from the – er – woman herself?' Zeuslove said.

'Odinstoy?' Faringdon said. 'Have you anything to say to these accusations?'

Odinstoy said, 'I did lie. I lied when I said Freeman Perry was my son's father. I lied because I didn't dare to tell the truth.'

Faringdon said, 'Oh?' while the Archpriest said, 'Oh, nonsense!'

Affie, still standing, was astonished.

'Might I ask,' Faringdon said, 'if this Perry isn't the father, who is?'

Odinstoy said, 'Odin.'

Going Up

The Archpriest was pleased. 'That is, quite simply, blasphemy.'

'Oh?' Faringdon was enjoying himself more and more. 'Don't you teach that several human heroes were fathered by Gods? Herakles, for instance? And wasn't Alexander the Great fathered by a God?'

'When that is concluded by due process of the temple,' said the Archpriest. 'When that conclusion is reached by a council of experts, who have heard all the evidence. It is not for someone like this – for a layperson—'

'An ex-bonder, I believe you were going to say,' Faringdon put in. 'Odinstoy isn't a layperson, is she? She's a God-speaker. Surely that makes her an expert in this field?'

The Archpriest ignored him, closing his eyes and brushing Faringdon's remark aside with a gesture of his hand. 'It is not open for a layperson, unrecognised by the Church of Mars, to declare that a God fathered her child – simply because it's expedient for her schemes.'

'You've made serious allegations against Odinstoy,'

Faringdon said. 'If, as you say, she's a thief and child-abductor, have you involved the police? Or do you simply prefer to use the information for self-publicity and political manoeuvring?'

'Obviously, I shall hand my file to the police at the first opportunity.'

'You mean, you haven't done it yet? Oh, but that means the story will stay in the news longer, doesn't it?'

'As yet, I've had no opportunity.'

'No opportunity? How long does— Oh, excuse me. I'm being told that we're out of time. Odinstoy! The final word to you, I think.'

Staring at the Archpriest, she said, 'I speak for Odin. And Mother Mars. I have done nothing wrong in Their eyes.' She leaned forward and raised her voice as the Archpriest tried to speak. 'I held on to my son when people wanted to take him from me. I set free those who should never have been *enslaved*. I did nothing wrong.'

In the control room, Affie stared at the screen, fascinated by the way this scene would look to those watching the broadcast across Mars. She was so caught in the moment that, when someone close beside her spoke, she started violently. Turning, she saw a man's face, so close she could see the pores in his skin. He whispered, 'You should get out of here as fast as you can.' It was Pope, the producer.

'Why?' Affie said. 'What's the matter?' But Pope went back to his desk.

Through the window, she could see Faringdon standing

and speaking to the Archpriest. Odinstoy was already on her way out of the studio.

Affie felt a pull at her sleeve, and turned to see a young woman with a head of bright-red and purple streaks – but it was merely dye, unlike the indigo lights rippling through Affie's hair. The woman's clothes were all black, and she wore a small silver knife and fork on a chain round her neck. 'Boss says I've got to take you out – quick, quick.'

'Why?' Affie demanded.

The woman pulled harder at her sleeve. 'The police! They're on their way to pick her up – come on! We'll give you a chance, anyway.'

Affie followed her. In the corridor outside the control room, they met Odinstoy. She was calling, 'John!'

John came running to join them, tugging Gift along behind him.

Affie wanted to hug Odinstoy and cry and apologise, admitting what she'd done – but there wasn't time. 'This way,' said the young woman, and led them briskly along confusing corridors, all alike, and not the same way they'd come earlier that day. Affie was relieved, though guilt still stabbed and pricked at her, like pins hidden in her clothes.

They went down through levels and came to parts of the building evidently not meant for public show – here were unpainted walls, uncovered concrete floors, shelves of bare, gaunt steel girders.

They came to a door. 'Your friends are outside,' the young woman said. 'We sent someone to warn them.' She opened the door.

There were people outside, standing in a crowd close to the door. Despite what the woman had said, Affie's first instinct was to shy away from them, trying to turn back – but Odinstoy caught her by the arm and shoved her out, before ushering the children through the door.

People crowded round them and Affie's heart beat faster – but then she saw Barley Taylor's face, and realised that these really were their friends, and not an angry mob set on lynching them for being runaway bonders and kidnappers. Serious young faces gazed at them, doe-eyed with awe.

'We heard,' they said.

'*We* believe you, Odinstoy.'

They'd watched on their phones and watches. One boy had a screen woven into the fabric of his sleeve.

'We know you wouldn't do anything wrong.'

'If it was Odin's will, what could you do?'

They were gathering round the children. 'Which is Odin's son?' one asked.

Barley said, 'The police are after you.' He was scared, but obviously also thrilled to find himself in the middle of something so exciting.

Odinstoy and Affie looked at each other. They knew only too well that the accusations of theft and abduction that the Archpriest had made against them were perfectly true. They might argue that the laws they'd broken were unfair and deserved to be broken, but they had still broken those laws. Now the fact had been broadcast across Mars, it was all too likely that the Martian police would be after them.

'I don't think we should talk to the police,' Affie said. Now they were accused, their IDs would be examined much more carefully. An expert, knowing what to look for, could tell that they'd been altered, and when, and possibly even by whom. Which would be bad luck for Bob Sing, back on Earth.

Then there were the other databases – such as the one that held records of all bonders. Bob hadn't had the time or the ability to alter that too. At the spaceport, on Earth, Odin Himself had saved them from being caught – or sheer luck had. But how many times would luck, or Odin, save them?

Why did we think we could get away with it? Affie thought. And why, *why* did I tell Jason so much – or anything at all? I'm a fool.

Gift was pulling at Odinstoy's arm, begging for her attention. She was staring right through Barley Taylor, staring at nothing, hearing nothing, while they all waited.

'Odinstoy,' Affie said. 'What shall we do?' All she could think of was to go back to the Taylors' place – where else could they go? – and sit there and wait for the police to come.

Odinstoy didn't answer. She was facing the knowledge that her treacherous God was finished with her. She had served His purpose, had come to Mars and called up Mother Mars – and now it could be that He would give her no more help.

'Odinstoy,' Barley said. 'What are we going to do?'

She came back to herself, saw their faces all watching her. She felt Gift tugging at her arm, and crouched down to hug him. 'Gift *is* mine,' she said. 'He *is* Odin's son. But they won't believe me. If the police take us, they'll send us back to Earth. They'll imprison me, they may hang me, and they'll give my son back to the people who stole him from me. They'll teach him to forget me. And Affie – at best, she'll be bonded again. They may hang her too. For helping me.'

And serve me right, Affie thought. It's all my fault. But she didn't want to hang. Her hand, she discovered, was rubbing at her throat.

There was silence. Then a girl whispered, 'Odin will help you.'

'If He chooses. But I'm Odin's Toy. He may have tired of me.'

'No!' they said. 'He won't have. No!'

Barley said, 'We shouldn't stay here. We should get going.'

'Where?' Affie asked, alarmed. 'If we go to your place, or to Osbourne, they'll know where to find us.'

'No,' Barley said, and looked at the others around him. 'We'll go up!'

Laughter broke out on their faces.

'Yeah!'

'Up!'

'Towards Odin – towards the High One!'

'What do you mean?' Affie said, but they were all moving off, bundling down the narrow yard in a crowd,

Gift and John clinging to Odinstoy. Affie had to go too. She felt as if she was carrying a hard, heavy lump in her belly: it was pure dread.

They were led along the back alleys, the delivery ways, through holes in boundary fences. Affie wished that she hadn't dressed in new, expensive clothes. Considering that everywhere in Mars was under cover, it was still remarkably dirty. And then she thought: Why am I still worrying about clothes? After what I've done? She realised just what a big fool she was.

People around her were still laughing and chattering about going up. Affie looked up into the dome overhead. It was so vast, its curve was hardly visible. It was divided into hexagonal bubbles and faintly threaded with walkways. She said, weakly, 'We're going up there?'

A girl next to her nodded, and then they were squeezing through another hole in a fence, and there was no time for explanations.

They crowded into a dirty yard, cluttered with plastic boxes and old plastic wrapping and even a few clumps of wild grass. At the head of the line, people seemed to be going into a door. Faces were turning to look at her.

'Where's Freewoman Atkinson?'

'Freewoman – you should come here.'

Affie went forward, edging past people who patted her arm and smiled. When she reached the front, she saw that the door opened into a lift built into a corner of the building – a rough sort of lift, the kind used simply for moving goods, though it was small. It seemed a strange place to put a lift. Odinstoy was already inside, together with John, Gift and Barley.

Reluctantly, Affie stepped into the lift. Immediately, the doors closed.

The lift rose upwards, with only slight shaking. Affie remembered how high, high above the dome had seemed, and her breathing shortened. She'd never been scared of heights – or had never thought she was – but then, she'd never been in a tiny box before, rising steadily into the sky towards thread-like walkways suspended above nothing.

In one corner, Odinstoy leaned, with Gift and John leaning against her. Her face was calm, but closed, and she stared at nothing. Perhaps she was talking to Odin.

Barley leaned in another corner. He held up a square card, showing it to Affie. 'We've all got these passes,' he said. 'Shouldn't have, but we have. One of the guys' dads works in maintenance, and he made loads of copies. Means we can get up there whenever we like.' He jerked his head towards the unseen, distant roof of the dome, towards which they were still rising. 'We can drink, smoke –' he shrugged '– You know . . .'

Odinstoy said nothing. Affie thought: How very, very – well, *bonderish*. When she'd been free and rich, she hadn't had to sneak off to drink and smoke and 'you know'. She could do whatever she liked, whenever she liked. Because, she suddenly realised, no one had cared.

The lift stopped and the door opened. Barley walked out onto a small grey platform. Odinstoy followed, going to the rail at the edge and looking over. Gift was with her, quite fearless, as he looked down between the panels. John, only a little hesitant, was next.

Affie hesitated at the door, peering out. She didn't think she could go out there. But they were looking back at her, waiting for her. 'Is it safe?'

Barley looked puzzled. ''S nobody about,' he said.

Affie was looking at the grey, steel platform she had to step onto – it had holes in it! – and at the spindly rails. 'Does it sway about and shake?'

Barley stamped, and then jumped, making a clashing sound. The platform did shudder. Gift shrieked with laughter; John looked scared, but then laughed.

Affie took a step back into the lift – which, she remembered, was suspended in a shaft. She darted forward again, just as the lift doors closed in her face.

They opened again. Barley had opened them from outside. 'The others want to come up,' he said. 'It's safe, honest. It sways a bit because it's stronger that way.'

Odinstoy came, took Affie's arm, and towed her out of the lift. Behind her, the doors closed and the lift descended.

Affie was frozen in the centre of the walkway, trying not to think about its filigree fragility, and all the distance below her feet.

'You don't understand about engineering,' Barley said. 'The domes give and bend all the time. They give with the wind, they flex in the heat and cold. If the walkways didn't give a bit, the domes would break them. But they're safe – look.' He strode out along a walkway ahead of them, his feet clanging. Beneath them, the walkway quivered. Gift ran after him, looking back for Odinstoy and the others.

Barley turned to look back. 'See? They've been up here for years – they've never fallen down. And we're up here all the time. Come on.'

They followed him. At first Affie would take only tiny steps, keeping to the centre of the walkway, terrified by its quivering. The path was slung across the vast width of the dome, and she closed her eyes, convinced that her next step was somehow going to pitch her over the waist-high rail and send her whirling, over and over, down to the ground below. Or perhaps to splat onto one of the mono-tubes that passed beneath them.

But after some minutes, because she had no choice, she grew bolder. The platform might tremble, but it didn't collapse. She hadn't fallen over the rail yet. And if John and Gift could be at ease up here, so could she be. Her steps became longer; she kept her eyes open, and looked up at the huge hexagonal bubbles above her – so close and so big that she wouldn't have been able to tell what shape they were, if she hadn't already known. As yet, though, she didn't dare do more than glance down.

Barley brought them to a place where the narrow walk-way widened into a platform, which was scattered with cardboard boxes, bubble-wrap, even old blankets and cush-ions. There were discarded drinks and food cartons. Affie looked at it all with distaste, but Barley sat down, and the two younger boys gleefully joined him, burrowing into the rubbish and throwing it at each other.

'This is where we all come,' he said. 'Great, isn't it? They'll never find you here.'

Affie looked round, wanting to believe him, but . . . it was a horrible place. Dirty, uncomfortable, and scary. Chilly too. As night drew on, it would be even colder. And if it was where they all came, then many, many people must know about that. It only needed one to have seen them on their way here, or one to tell . . . She wanted to stamp her foot and shout, but didn't – because stamping would make the platform shake, and because it was all her fault that they'd had to come up here. She thought, with sudden fondness, of their tiny flat in Osbourne. It had been so cramped, but it had been theirs, and they'd been free . . . She grieved inside: Oh, you fool, you *fool* . . .

'We'll freeze,' she said. She *had* to say that. They would freeze, and they had children with them.

Barley snatched up the dirty blanket and some bubble-wrap, and held them out to her. She just looked at him. 'And where are we supposed to – relieve ourselves?'

'Oh, there's a toilet back there. Come and look.' He walked off across the shaking platform, to a small grey shed at the back of it. Odinstoy, Gift and John followed him curiously and Affie went after them, distastefully picking her way through the rubbish, and not liking the way the platform felt beneath her feet. She still feared it was going to break loose of its fastening and crash down, smashing into other walkways and tube lines on its way.

The shed, when they reached it, housed a tiny sonic shower, a toilet, and a very small kitchen with a sink, a fridge, and a hob. 'Everything you need,' Barley said.

Affie nodded. 'Yes,' she said meekly. 'Very nice. Thank you.'

'Look at this!' Barley said. He led them out of the little rest room, and to the side of it. There, they were at the very edge of the dome. They could touch the giant hexagonal frames that held the huge bubbles. Odinstoy reached out and touched one of the bubbles. It was taut and hardly moved. Dimly, through its thickness, they saw the clouds.

'They put spider silk into the steel,' Barley said. 'There's nothing stronger.'

It seemed strange to be there, so close to the dome's wall – like standing at the end of the world.

One great hexagon had been replaced by a door, or porthole. 'That's how you get outside the dome,' Barley said. 'It's an airlock.' He pressed a button beside it, and with a buzz of machinery, the lock started to open.

'Don't!' Affie cried, imagining red, poisonous Martian air pouring in.

'That's only the inner lock!' Barley said scornfully. 'We go and sit in there, sometimes. You have to open the outer lock before there's any danger.' He pressed the button and the lock closed again. 'They think only maintenance men can get up here,' he said, and giggled.

Affie looked at the rubbish strewn around the platform. 'They must *know* you can get up here.'

Barley shrugged. 'Ah, well. They know, but – you know.'

The walkway and platform began to ring and quiver beneath them, and Affie looked round in alarm. Was their combined weight causing it to break at last? 'It's the others coming from the lift,' Barley said, and Affie felt a spurt of irritation at the thought of being joined by all those excitable, chattering, puppy-eyed devotees of Odinstoy – until she thought of being up here alone with Odinstoy. Then she wanted the whole gang to hurry along to join them as quickly as they could.

Barley led the way back to the main part of the platform. 'You see, nobody can come up here without you knowing about it.'

Odinstoy seated herself on the floor among the old boxes. 'Will the maintenance teams come here?'

'No,' the boy said. 'Not for a long time, anyway. They work their way round the domes all the time – they won't be back here for a while.'

The others came up – making the platform shake and clang – and settled themselves among the rubbish. They were all young. Some produced sandwiches, drinks, bags of snacks, and placed them in front of Odinstoy – who got up and walked away. She went to the edge of the platform and leaned on the rail.

Affie stood watching her, wanting to join her, but afraid of what might be said. She was afraid, also, to go so close to the rail. She thought Odinstoy looked unhappy – well, of *course* she was unhappy! And it was her, Affie's, fault.

She couldn't remember ever feeling so bad about some-thing that was happening to someone else; but she couldn't think of anything to say.

Odinstoy turned, still leaning on the rail. She said, 'How did the Archpriest know?'

Affie couldn't answer and couldn't look at her. She turned away, looking back towards the others. Her stom-ach felt sick.

'Affie. How did he find out?'

Affie tried to look at her, but couldn't. She felt her face warming. 'I don't—'

Odinstoy grabbed her upper arm and pulled her against the rail. Affie thought she was going to fall over it, and grabbed frantically both at the rail and at Odinstoy. She saw below her – so much space . . . and roofs and roads. Her breath stopped.

'Who told him?' Odinstoy asked, close at her ear.

'Earth Has Officially
Demanded . . .'

'We'd like to ask you some questions, if that's possible, Freeman Blackmore.'

Thorsgift had known they would come. He stood aside and let them in, while feeling as if a heavy weight was pressing on his chest, making it hard to breathe.

He led them through the entrance hall, with its shrine to his family's ancestors, and upstairs to the family room. There he invited the policemen to sit down, and asked if they would like a drink.

'Thank you, Freeman, but no.'

'Anything to eat? And the facilities are through there if you need them.' Odin Himself had said that a guest should be offered a chance to wash, eat and drink before anything else.

'Thank you, Freeman, no. Can we get on?'

They all sat a little awkwardly, even Thorsgift, who was in his own home.

'We understand, Freeman, that you made a trip to

Earth – that it was you, in fact, who recruited Odinstoy Atkinson to be God-speaker here?'

You know I did, Thorsgift wanted to say. 'I did – it was me, yes.'

'You're aware of the accusations that have been made against the God-speaker?' said the other policeman.

Thorsgift felt ill. He nodded.

'Have you anything to say about those accusations, Freeman?'

Thorsgift sighed. It had happened, what he'd always dreaded. They'd been found out. These policeman knew what he'd done. They just wanted him to admit it. Why not do that, as they were waiting and hoping for him to do? But he'd be admitting Odinstoy's and Affie's guilt too, and he didn't know what they'd said to the police, if anything. Then, too, there were the people back on Earth who'd helped them – Bob Sing, who'd altered databases; and the doctor, Markus, who'd removed ID tags from their bodies. He hardly knew them, but somehow it seemed worse to incriminate a near-stranger, who'd never so much as spoken to him harshly, than a close friend.

'I know nothing about it,' he said.

They stared at him: long, blank stares that went on and on. He felt his heart thump, and his face flushed slightly.

'Nothing?' one of them said.

'You didn't know that Millington was a runaway bonder?'

Thorsgift swallowed, with some difficulty. If he answered no to that question, he would make things a great deal worse for himself when, inevitably, they were able to prove that he *had* known.

'I think I'd better see a lawyer,' he said. Wasn't that request, in itself, an admission of guilt? He felt even more ill.

'Did you know that Millington and Odinstoy weren't married, and the child wasn't theirs?'

'I don't want to answer these questions without a lawyer.'

'Do you know where Odinstoy is now?'

So they didn't know where she was! 'I genuinely have no idea,' Thorsgift said, with relief, 'and I want a lawyer.'

'How did they find out?' Odinstoy asked again.

Affie, with the drop into the heart of the dome below her, was too scared to answer.

'You told Jason,' Odinstoy said.

Fear made Affie want to deny it; guilt made her want to admit it. 'Please—!' she said, with tears starting. She meant: Please don't throw me over.

'You told Jason. Odin tells me so. I know you did.'

'I'm sorry!' Affie started crying, crying hard; partly from fear, but also because the guilt and dread was too heavy to hold inside any more. 'Oh, I'm so sorry, Odinstoy! I won't do it again, I won't—'

Odinstoy laughed, and let her go.

Affie backed off from the rail and, for a few moments,

was crying too much to know what was going on around her. Then she wiped tears from her eyes and, still sobbing, looked round. Odinstoy was sitting on the platform, leaning her back against the panels that formed the safety rail. Affie knelt by her. Nothing could have made her lean against those panels.

'Odinstoy, I am sorry, I am, I really am. I'm so sorry – I didn't think he'd tell—'

Odinstoy laughed again. 'You're a bloody fool.'

'I am! And I've done for us all, and I'm so—' She sobbed again, crying into her hands. Two other feelings came worming through the upset. One was surprise: I really am sorry! The other was puzzlement. Odinstoy didn't seem to be angry.

'I thought I could trust him. I thought he loved me – honestly, Odinstoy, I wouldn't have told him if I'd thought—'

'Stupid,' Odinstoy said. 'Lazy. Gormless. Selfish. Spoiled. Useless. Brat.'

Affie was startled, but then realised that the 'brat' Odinstoy was talking about wasn't Gift, but her. Even so, Odinstoy still didn't seem angry.

She also realised that Odinstoy was right. She was all those things. Because she was all those things, she'd let Odinstoy down – and Odinstoy was the only friend she'd ever had. Her mother had abandoned her, her father had shot himself and left her to be bonded; and all her friends on Earth had dumped her as soon as she'd lost her money.

And Jason? He hadn't even been her friend for ten

minutes. She was such a fool, she couldn't recognise a creep, even when the creep was as big a creep as Jason.

'Odinstoy – what can I do?'

'Nothing.'

'But if there's anything I can do – I'm so sorry, I am – I'll do anything I can to make it—'

Odinstoy slid across the platform floor towards her. Affie flinched, thinking she was about to be hit, but she was only hit by Odinstoy's arms reaching out and wrapping round her. Amazed, Affie found herself hugged. 'Forget it. It wasn't your fault.'

Affie, her face warm and muffled in Odinstoy's shoulder, was too surprised to cry. Not her fault? 'Then whose fault—?'

'Odin's.'

'It's Odin's—?' Affie couldn't understand it.

But Odinstoy's hands stroked her back soothingly. She said, 'There is love for you.' Affie melted into broken-hearted, but relieved, sobs.

'*The controversy surrounding the Odin-worshipping canton of Osbourne, and their new God-speaker, deepens.*'

The voice of the announcer came from the speakers hidden in the walls as Barley searched for food in the kitchen. He snatched apples and pears from the bowl on the table, stuffing it into his kit-bag along with packs of cheesy nibbles, nuts and corn-chips.

'*Earth has officially demanded the return of Odinstoy and her companion to face charges of theft and abduction. They*

*could also face charges here on Mars of illegal entry, although,
as yet, their whereabouts are unknown . . .'*

Barley took a large chopping knife from the metallic
strip on the wall, pulled open a drawer, and selected a
cleaver. He dropped both kitchen tools into his bag and
took another look round. Deciding there was nothing else
he could take without it being missed, he carried his kit-
bag from the kitchen and into the glass-fronted hall at the
front of the house. There he stowed it behind a bench
where he could collect it on his way out. He wandered
back into the house, to find his mother and father.

They were in the family room. His mother was standing at the window with her arms folded, watching the
police search the garden. His father was sitting on the sofa,
looking miserable. Maybe he was watching the broadcast
on the screen, or maybe he was thinking his own thoughts.

I ought to tell them what I'm doing, Barley thought
– but if he did, they'd insist on his telling the police everything he knew. 'It's for the Gods to decide,' they would
say. Then the police would arrest Odinstoy and Affie, they'd
be sent back to Earth, the little boy would be sent away
from his mother . . . Perhaps this was what the Gods
wanted, but Barley didn't think you had to tamely go along
with that, and Odin wouldn't hold it against them if they
fought to the end. Odin planned to go down fighting at
the End of the World, even though He knew the fight
couldn't be won.

He went over to his mother and stood beside her. The
police were hunting through the small orchard, looking in

the little tool-shed, and going down into the underground chamber that housed the irrigation system.

Seeing her son, Freewoman Taylor sighed, and said, 'They're searching the bedrooms too.'

Barley shrugged. 'They have to do their jobs, Mum.'

'I know. Is it true, what they're saying about Odinstoy?'

'No,' he said.

'They want to speak to you, anyway.'

'I've got nothing to tell them.'

'You went with her to the television place.'

'Oh! No – I lost her.' His mother looked at him. 'There were so many people,' he said. 'Trying to get on the same mono with us. We got split up. I don't know where she is now.'

'Then you must tell them that,' his mother said.

'I will!' he said. 'I'll go and find whoever's in charge now and tell them.' And, nodding firmly, he left the room, picked up his kit-bag, and made his way through the grounds to the mono-link, walking past policemen as he went. The best hiding place was right out in the open, wasn't it? So he'd heard it said. If he just walked boldly, openly to the mono-rail, everyone would suppose that he had nothing to hide, and would let him go.

It worked brilliantly until he reached the entrance to the mono, where a policeman, a big man in a dark-red uniform, blocked his way.

'Would you mind telling me where you're going, Freechild?'

'Just – out,' Barley said.

'We'd appreciate it if you'd cooperate with us by staying within the dome, please, Freechild.'

'It's our dome,' Barley said. 'I can go if I want to.'

The policeman gave him a long, considering stare, and Barley felt like curling up.

'We're simply asking you to cooperate with our enquiries, Freechild. I'm sure you want to do that.'

'Of course,' Barley said, and felt himself begin to sweat as he noticed another policeman strolling over to join them. 'But I shan't be long – I shall be back in a few minutes.'

He expected some response, but there was only another long stare. The second policeman stopped beside the first, arms behind his back, and he stared too. Barley couldn't tell what they were thinking. They scared him.

'Would you mind showing us what you have in the bag, Freechild?' the first asked.

'No! I mean – why? It's nothing.'

'Then you won't mind showing us.'

'I don't see why—'

The second policeman said, 'We're asking you politely, Freechild.'

Barley was thinking frantically, trying to remember exactly what he had in the bag – food and knives. What explanation could he give? What would they think? Policemen were supposed to be stupid, weren't they?

If he refused to open the bag, what would they do? Arrest him? Could they really arrest him for refusing to open a bag?

The second policeman reached out and took the bag, saying, 'Let's have a look.' Barley let him do it.

Both policemen looked into the bag and exchanged glances.

'We're having a picnic!' Barley said. 'I'm going to meet friends, we—'

The second policeman said, 'I think you'd better come back to the house with me, Freechild.'

'But it's only for a picnic!' Barley said wildly.

'Back at the house, we'll phone your friends, and speak to your parents, and if your story checks out, you can be on your way,' said the policeman, and gestured for Barley to walk ahead of him.

Barley turned and began the walk back to the house, feeling sick. He didn't want to speak to his parents, he didn't want to have to explain why he didn't feel like phoning his friends about the picnic. He wondered if running – finding somewhere to hide – would do any good.

He kept on walking.

'Earth has officially demanded the return of Odinstoy and her companion . . .'

Affie and a girl called Dorrie were watching the broadcast on the little screen of Dorrie's phone. Odinstoy's face, clipped from the film of her at the temple, filled the little space.

'I don't want to go back to Earth,' Affie said.

'Don't worry,' Dorrie said. 'It'll take years. It always does with anything like this. My dad always says so. He says they appoint committees to look into it, and then report, and then discuss the report, and then they have another investigation – years and years it could take, before they send you back.'

Well, that sounded all right, except – 'But where will we be, Odinstoy and me? While they're doing all the investigating and reporting? Will we be in jail?'

'I don't know,' Dorrie admitted.

'They won't be sent back,' said another girl, called Nike. She spoke as if she knew for certain. 'People won't let them.'

Several of those seated among the rubbish on the platform nodded.

'Osbourne's on your side,' an older girl, a young woman, said. 'You're one of us. And a lot of other people think the same way.'

'Why should we jump just because Earth whistles?' said a boy, Cedar, and there was louder agreement.

'Affie should never have been bonded – she was born free!'

'And Gift really *is* Odinstoy's child, so of course he should be with her!'

'Only Earth would make laws like that!'

'Is Barley back yet?' someone asked; and then people were twisting round, and craning to see past other people, and asking had they seen Barley? Had he said when he was coming back?

'He's been gone a long time,' said the girl who'd asked after him.

'Where's Odinstoy?' Affie asked. Odinstoy had risen and walked off towards the back of the platform at least an hour ago.

John was scuffling among the rubbish with Gift, somewhere behind Affie. Now he popped up at her shoulder, fending off Gift while he said, 'She's in the airlock.'

'Why?' Affie turned towards him. He shrugged, and then Gift pulled him over backwards.

Perhaps Odinstoy was upset? It had been a long, cold, miserable night, and Odinstoy had Gift to worry about . . . Maybe things were getting too much even for her. And Odinstoy had been so good to her, hugging her even when everything was her fault . . . Twisting to her knees, Affie said, 'Shall I go to her?'

John held Gift down for a moment. 'No,' he said. 'She's talking to Odin.'

Affie sat again, and everyone subsided, looking at each other with a touch of awe.

'Has anybody got any more food?'

Odinstoy was in the airlock. The door onto the platform stood open, but she sat hugging her knees, on the other side, closer to Mars. At her feet lay the phone that someone had bought her – had it been the Taylors, Thorsgift, Fitzpatrick? People were always giving her things. A gift always looks for a return.

Her eyes were shut. There was nothing to see except the steel of the lock's walls and floor and, outside the door, a glimpse of the rubbish-strewn platform. She could hear, faintly, the chatter of her 'Bonders' as they repeated their hopes, as if repeating them could make them come true. The squeakings and creakings of the dome's frame was louder.

In her mind, she was calling and calling to Odin. She made His image in her mind, building it carefully, going over and over it: the Hanged God, with His tongue forced from His mouth by the throttling rope around His neck. The Wise God, with His single eye, because He had given His other for knowledge . . . Odin, look on this world with Your sighted eye, and on the next world with Your blind eye, and advise me, help me . . .

Odin, I need You. Come to me. Speak to me.

She waited for an answer to rise from the depths of her mind. Any answer, good or bad, any word from the God . . .

Nothing. Just the inconsequential chatter of thoughts: What's going to happen to Gift? I'm hungry. Will we be hung? And Gift, Gift, Gift . . .

Will the Perrys take him back? Will they still love him when he grows older, when he isn't a pretty little boy? By then, he won't remember me. He'll never know that I loved him.

She tried to concentrate, to stifle all thought except thought of Odin, the Raging One, the Treacherous God . . .

Odin came. She felt Him close around her, felt Him rise inside her. She swayed forward and almost sobbed with relief.

Here it ends, said Odin. *Come home to Me.*

Gift, she said. Gift.

Bring Him.

No. Not Gift. And I can't leave him alone.

He won't be alone.

Affie? No. I can't leave him.

Then bring him. Now you must come to Me.

She swayed forward again, covering her face with her hands. I can't. This I can't do.

Why stay? Odin asked. *I've done with you. Stay, and you'll be sent back to Earth. You know this. Your son will be taken from you. You know this.*

I know, I know . . .

You'll be alone, imprisoned. I shall never come to you again. I shall burst no locks. And Affie – if you care for her—

I care.

You know what will happen to her. Prison: a hard time. And when that's done, her bond will be sold – if anyone will buy it. She'll be cheap. She'll be treated like something cheap.

Odinstoy's head remained bowed into her hands. She drew a long breath. I knew there would be a price. I accepted.

Then come to me. I offer you a kindness.

If I come, will You let Gift stay? Will You guard him?

My bargain with you is done. I make no more.

Let Gift stay. Please.

Then let Gift stay. I'll tell you his life. He'll go back to the Perrys and he'll never hear your name. He'll forget you. He'll own bonders, and use them; he'll despise them. He'll be free. Isn't that what you wish for him – that he'll be free?

Odinstoy felt as if a long sharp spear was being slowly forced through her, the pain sharp and endless . . . Odin forced the spear through Himself when He hung on the World Tree, sacrificing Himself to Himself, to learn the secrets of death.

But, said Odin, *birds forsake chicks touched by men. Maybe the Perrys won't touch your son again. They'll give him to strangers. Or they'll say, 'The child must follow the mother,' and bond him.*

He would be alive.

Then leave him to his fate, however woven. You must come to Me.

I can't.

You're strong. You were, always. You have the strength to live through the loss of your son. The strength to be without Me. The strength to be bonded again, to be a nothing. I salute your strength.

Don't leave me!

Then come to Me.

I can't, I can't . . .

But Odin was gone.

She opened her eyes. She'd always known that Odin would, one day, desert her . . . When you accepted Odin's inspiration, that was the deal you made. She'd always imagined that, when the betrayal came, she could accept it – but it was like trying to imagine falling hard on a steel floor. However carefully you used your imagination and memory, you could never recreate the true bruising, jarring impact. However often you'd prepared yourself, the reality always hurt more than you could have expected.

When people asked her to speak for Odin in future – if they ever did – would she lie, pretend she heard a voice she no longer heard?

But who would ask her to speak for Odin in a prison on Earth?

She thought: I have to go to Odin.

And take Gift?

She twisted, bent forward, in a spasm of revulsion and rejection. Gift must stay.

Would she go to Odin and leave Gift behind? Leave him, to be pulled and shoved this way and that, without her to stand guard and protect?

Again, the twisting spasm. She had to stay, but must go. Had to leave Gift behind, but must take him.

She sat up straight and thought, coldly and clearly. Had she had a mother to protect her? Her mother had been sold on while Odinstoy had still been a small child. She hadn't named her child, or left anything of herself with her daughter except a votive medallion of Freya. Odinstoy had nevertheless grown up. So did thousands of other bonder children. So must Gift.

It hadn't been what Odinstoy had wanted or planned. But Odin had left her – as she'd always known He would. That was her fate.

She would go to Odin, and leave Gift behind.

She picked up the camera, held it before her face, and began filming.

When Thorsgift came back to Osbourne, everyone knew, within half an hour. E-mails flew, phone calls were made. 'How did he look? Were the police with him? Does he know where Odinstoy is?'

When Thorsgift was seen walking towards Osbourne's shrine to Thor, the texts and e-mails flew again, and several people felt a need to thank Thor for something.

They allowed Thorsgift to make his offering to his God, and to stand in prayer, palms held up. Then, as he turned away, they went to meet him. Rebecca touched his arm. 'How are you, love?'

He looked tired, they all noticed that.

'Was it awful?' Ingrid Woodhouse asked. 'What did they ask you?'

Thorsgift shook his head. He didn't want to talk. The memory of the long hours of questioning was too raw and painful. 'Say nothing,' his lawyer had advised him; and he had gritted his teeth and obeyed.

Had he known? Had he known Affie's ID was false? Had he known they weren't married? Where was Odinstoy now?

No comment; no comment. Now all Thorsgift wanted to do was sleep, though he doubted he'd be able to.

Inga Bailey came running around the duck-pond to join them. Breathlessly, she said, 'They know where Odinstoy is! They've just announced it!'

'Where?' Rebecca said.

Someone switched on their phone. Even as Inga pointed into the air, a voice from the phone said, '*Earth has officially demanded . . .*' People were looking up, bewildered, towards the roof of the dome.

'The maintenance tracks,' Inga said. 'She's up on the maintenance tracks. In the main dome above Ares. They know she's there – "information received", they said – and they're going to fetch her down.'

Malfunction

Odinstoy was telling off her ancestor string. 'This blue bead—'

'Is for your great-grandmother,' Affie said, eager to show that she remembered, and was grateful still to be loved by Odinstoy.

'Who is it for?' Odinstoy asked.

John whispered to Gift, who said, 'Great-Great-Grandmother!'

Odinstoy smiled, and stroked John's hair briefly, before kissing Gift. 'I know nothing about her,' she said. 'Not even a name. She was a bonder and was sold away from her children. This locket – look, it has a picture in it . . .'

Gift peered at the hologram of a woman that smiled at him from the locket.

'That's my grandmother, and your great-grandmother.'

'Is that a picture of her?' John asked.

'Yes,' Odinstoy said, and Affie kept quiet, though she knew that sometimes Odinstoy said no to this question, and didn't really know the answer. 'I don't know her name either. She was a bonder too.'

Gift pointed at the little medallion and said, 'What?'

'That—' Odinstoy began, but was startled into open-mouthed silence by yells and screams. The platform and walkways shook beneath them, to a clangour of running feet. Affie clutched at a rail and squeaked in fright.

Odinstoy got to her feet, said to Gift and John, 'Stay,' and moved towards the noise. Cedar Campbell and another lad scrambled up quickly and moved in front of her. Whatever was causing the uproar they, as her self-appointed Bonders, would not let her face it alone.

Other Bonders were running towards them along the walkways, from both directions, looking back and shouting. 'Police!' the nearest yelled at Cedar.

And looking beyond the Bonders, they saw the dark-red uniforms of the police coming in single file along the narrow walkways.

'They've come for Odinstoy!'

Cedar swung round on Odinstoy. 'Get back – get out of sight!'

'There's nowhere to hide,' she said, but he wasn't listening. He was pushing people along the walkways. 'Hold 'em off! Block the way! They're not getting through!'

Several Bonders hurried eagerly into place. The walkways were barely wide enough for two men to pass; four big lads on either side blocked them completely. And these big lads suddenly had weapons – produced from pockets, or bags, or from amongst the rubbish they'd been sitting in: wrenches, cleavers, solid spade handles, hoes.

The police, seeing trouble ahead, came to a halt. The

big sergeant in the lead said, 'We are here on police business, to arrest Odinstoy and her companion, Affroditey Millington, on charges of theft and abduction. Let us by.'

Cedar said, 'No.' He was scared, his voice shook, and the word came out as a dry squeak. So he repeated it, more loudly. 'No!'

The sergeant eyed him, then relaxed from his upright, official pose. Ducking his head forward, he said, 'Don't play daft games, son. We're going to arrest her. It's only a matter of when.'

'She's done nothing wrong,' Cedar said.

'Do your job,' said the taller boy beside him. 'Investigate. Then you'll find out.'

The sergeant looked weary and sighed. 'Stand aside.' He took a step forward, and Cedar raised his cleaver. Behind him, various other weapons were held at the ready.

The sergeant backed off and stood looking at them. 'You're obstructing the police in the performance of their duty—' There were cat-calls and jeers. 'That's an arrestable offence!'

'She didn't do anything wrong!' Cedar said.

'I'm asking you to stand aside and allow me to carry out my duty.'

Cedar couldn't speak. His heart was banging hard, seemingly on the back of his teeth. He'd never done anything so bad before. His parents would be furious. Briefly, he thought of standing aside and letting the police take Odinstoy. It would be the end of so much . . . But after all, his life would carry on much as before . . .

The boy beside him said, 'We're not going anywhere. You're not coming through.'

From behind them came a cheer, and a chant of 'Mother Mars! Mother Mars!'

Cedar took a long, shuddering breath. He was so glad the decision had been made for him.

The sergeant, his eyes on Cedar and the boy beside him, spoke into his watch. 'We've met resistance. We're coming down.' He paused, listening to someone speak in his ear. 'No – kids. Rich kids. Armed. We're coming down.' With a lingering stare at Cedar, he turned and signalled to the men behind him to withdraw.

For a moment, Cedar and the other Bonders watched the dark-red backs of the police marching away; then they whooped and danced in triumph, making the walkways quiver and clang. Those behind ran back to the platform, taking the news.

'They've gone!'

'We chased them off!'

'We won!'

Affie felt a tremulous pleasure, a first hope – she looked at Odinstoy, to see what she thought. Odinstoy was seated, hugging Gift and John to her, her head bent. As Affie came closer, Odinstoy looked up and said, 'They haven't gone.'

They settled down on the platform again, though some of the Bonders posted themselves on watch, on the walkways. People passed food and drink: biscuits and packets of snacks, cans of fizzy drinks, a few sandwiches.

'We've made them *think*,' someone said. 'They can't just come barging up here now.'

'They have to listen!' a boy said. 'When they see how people feel, they'll have to listen!'

'Lots of people are behind us!'

As she listened, Affie watched Odinstoy, who was sitting with the two children, staring at nothing. A heavy feeling of despair settled under Affie's breastbone. What are we waiting for? she thought.

It was never warm, up there on the platform, close to the roof of the dome. As the Martian night returned, it grew colder yet.

A voice rose out of the thickening dusk, its tone crowing. 'They still haven't come back, have they?'

Gift started to grizzle, because he was cold, tired, and hungry. Affie curled up on her side in the rubbish – something she'd thought she'd never do – and tried to sleep.

When day came again, the food was finished. A boy came back from the walkways, saying, 'They've gone! We drove them off!'

'Don't be stupid,' Cedar snapped. He was feeling stupid. 'They won't be waiting where we can see them! They'll be down at the bottom, outside the lifts.'

'You mean, we can't go down?' an indignant voice asked.

'What is this, a game? Well, that team we're playing against? They're the *police*.'

Odinstoy got to her feet. She stood still, in silence, and everyone on the platform fell silent and turned to look at her. She said, 'You must leave, all of you. Go home. Go home now.'

Some people looked round uncertainly, even started to get up, as if they were considering it. Cedar, who had been thinking of leaving himself, immediately changed his mind. 'And leave you on your own? They'll just come up and arrest you.'

'I'm in Odin's hands,' she said. 'Leave it to Him.'

Cedar stood up. 'We can't go.' He looked round at the others. 'They'll only arrest us anyway.'

'Yeah!' another young man agreed, standing beside him.

Affie, chilled and shivering in the rubbish, couldn't stand listening to them any more. Sitting up, she said, 'Oh, you're so stupid! What are you going to do? Fight them with kitchen knives?'

'Yeah!' And there were whistles and cheers.

'We're fighting for *you*!' Cedar said indignantly.

'We're trapped up here! There's nowhere we can go – there's no room to fight!'

One of the bigger lads – she didn't know his name – pointed to where a walkway joined the platform. 'Perfect defensive position! Nobody can get by us there – we can hold them off for ever!'

'Oh, you think you're generals now?' Affie said. 'Such big men! Are you going to hold them off until we starve or until we freeze?'

The big lad's face turned ugly with anger. If she hadn't been Odinstoy's wife, he'd have shouted something at her. Instead he turned his back.

'Odin was a warrior,' Cedar said. 'He fought, even though He knew He'd be defeated in the end. He fought because you always have to fight!'

'Fight for what's right!' said the other boy, and began a sort of dance, hopping from one foot to the other, and punching his fists above his head.

Odinstoy lifted her head, and Affie thought she was going to speak, but others jumped up and joined in the dance, chanting 'Fight for what's right!' and 'Mother Mars!' The platform rang and clanged beneath them, making discordant music. They made too much noise for anyone to be heard.

Affie, angry at their stupidity, got to her feet with some idea of finding a quiet place away from their inane noise and bragging. That was hopeless, of course – where could she go? But perhaps she could get further away from the noisiest pests. She was looking round when she saw Odinstoy walking away towards the back of the platform, picking her way over people and through rubbish. She was holding Gift's hand, and John was following them.

Something made Affie afraid. She was about to go after them when, from below, a blaring yell nearly made her fall with shock. It resolved itself into words: '*This is the police. We want to question Odinstoy. Question her, that's all. If everyone comes down now, no one will be hurt, or arrested, except Odinstoy and Millington. We repeat*—'

Odinstoy looked back. That shout, those words, were the beginning of the end, she knew. It felt as if her heart, broken loose from its moorings inside her, was plummeting down a lift-shaft. Reaching back for John's hand, she drew him to her. Crouching, to be a little smaller than him, she looked him in the face, then drew his head down and kissed his brow. He looked at her solemnly. She said, 'John, I wish I had more time to be with you – I wish there was more time for you to be my son.'

He said, 'Am I your son?'

'Yes. As much as Gift is. I have two sons.'

He lunged and hugged her. She hugged him tight, but said into his neck, 'I wish we had more time, but we haven't. John, I need you to do something for me. Will you do something for me?'

'Yes!'

Pulling a little away from him, she gave him something – the little card from inside a phone. 'I need you to keep this for me – keep it safe, keep it for Gift. Will you?'

'Yes.'

'Give it to him when he's old enough . . .' She was standing, pulling away from him.

He held on to her sleeve. 'When?'

'When he's a man. When he's eighteen.'

She was pulling away.

'Don't go!' John said.

She pulled away from him, turned away.

Affie, looking round, couldn't see that people were rushing to obey the police. Some were leaning over the rails, jeering; most seemed stunned. She looked for Odinstoy again, and saw her talking to John. Affie moved towards them, picking her way through people sitting and lying and standing in huddled groups.

Then John looked round, and the expression on his face as it twisted into an open-mouthed sob was of such anguish that she pressed forward as quickly as she could.

Odinstoy, leading Gift by the hand, passed by the door of the washroom. That wasn't where she was going. She was going to the airlock! Reaching John, Affie grabbed his arm and took him on with her.

Odinstoy, ahead of her, reached the airlock – Affie's way and view was blocked by three girls going the other way. When she could see again, Odinstoy had caught Gift up in her arms and was hugging him. Affie took a running, clashing jump, to catch up with her more quickly – the boldest move she'd ever dared to make on the trembling platform. 'Odinstoy!'

Odinstoy didn't hear her – or anything. She had come to the moment of parting with Gift – Odin's Gift to her which, with His usual treachery, He was now taking away. She had made up her mind that it must be so: that Gift must remain behind, to make whatever sort of life he could.

But now – now she had lifted him into her arms for one last hug – now she couldn't let him go. Never mind that she had given John the message for him, never mind anything. She couldn't let him go – not when she knew how harsh and bitter life could be.

'Want to come with me?' she asked him. 'Want to come and see Odin?'

Gift, hugging her neck, said, 'Yes!'

She was lifting Gift into the airlock when Affie, appearing at her side, said, 'Toy, what are you doing?'

John, his face twisted with fear and uncertainty, backed off a few steps.

Odinstoy said, calmly, 'Go away, Affie.' She ducked to enter the airlock.

In her hand, as it rested for a moment on the edge of the airlock, Affie saw one of the copied cards: the passcards that opened the doors.

'Odinstoy! Stop!'

Odinstoy looked out of the lock. 'Come with us,' she said, as if proposing a day-trip to the beach.

Affie reached the entrance of the lock and leaned on it, looking inside. Gift was standing in the middle, his fingers in his mouth, waiting for his mother to take charge of him. He doesn't know, he doesn't understand, Affie thought. How could he? The brat was only four.

'Odinstoy,' Affie said. 'You can't. Don't.'

Odinstoy stared at her with those dark, intense eyes. 'Do you want to go back to Earth?'

Affie thought of the future waiting for her if she did, and it was like looking into a cold, dark fog.

'Come with us,' Odinstoy said. 'To Him. Freedom. A life of feasting.'

Affie's belief didn't go that deep. A life of feasting? It wasn't what she wanted. Neither was the life waiting for her on Earth, but at least that life would be real, if miserable.

'Gift!' Affie reached her arm into the airlock, reaching out to him. 'Come out of there!'

Gift took his fingers from his mouth, but looked at Odinstoy. Leaning in further, Affie said, 'Come here, Gift! Come here now!'

Uncertain, still looking at his mother, he took a step towards her – then Odinstoy held out her hand, and he went to her instead.

'Gift! You brat! Come here! – Odinstoy—' Tears were running down Affie's face. 'Don't do this. Please.'

'Odin called me.'

'But not Gift!'

'I won't leave him behind.'

'After all we went through to get him away, now you're going to kill him?'

'He'll be with me. With Odin.'

'Oh – bugger Odin!' Affie said. 'Gift! Come here!'

Gift knew something was wrong now, and he was scared. He tried to go to Affie, but was held back by his mother.

'Odinstoy,' Affie said, 'don't give up. If we have to go back to Earth – we'll be together.'

'They'll never let us be together again.'

'When we come out of prison—'

'They'll hang you.'

Affie's throat tightened and narrowed, as if the rope were already drawing close around it. She whispered, 'Then I'll be alive right up to the moment they do it! I won't do the job for them!'

Odinstoy looked surprised at that, even shocked, as if the idea that Affie could say anything that could surprise her was shocking.

Tears spilled from Affie's eyes, and a wail broke from her throat. Her face folded and twisted in a way that couldn't be beautiful. Her hair was full of indigo lights. She said, 'Oh, Odinstoy, don't leave me on my own!' She held out both arms, asking for a hug. 'Don't leave us alone, please don't!'

Odinstoy hesitated, then came to her, arms out to embrace her. Affie seized both her arms, grappled her and dragged her out of the airlock, hanging on when Odinstoy fought back, even though it hurt, hanging on with a fierceness and determination she hadn't known was in her.

They were clear of the lock, and scuffling on the hard platform, among crisp packets, cardboard and dusty bubble-wrap. They went over, Affie underneath, and the hard platform hurt and clanged, and breath was knocked out of her, but Affie still hung on. She cried out as Odinstoy knelt on her – but wrapped her fist in Odinstoy's shirt, and hung on, hung on. Her head clanged on the platform, it hurt, she saw white lights, and felt sick and giddy; but as her vision cleared, she had her arms clamped around Odinstoy's legs, and she glimpsed John, hand in hand with Gift, running away.

Affie heaved, and Odinstoy toppled, crashing and clanging onto the platform. From below, a voice boomed: '*If you come down, nobody will be hurt. We'll give a sympathetic hearing to your side of things. You'll have to come down—*'

'A sym – pa – thetic – hearing,' Affie panted.

Odinstoy, slowly sitting up, said nothing.

Affie drew a little away from her and dragged in some breath. 'I don't want to go back to Earth. But we'd be alive! Odin fought on, even when He knew He'd lost!'

'Odin has called me to Him.'

'Odin doesn't exist!' Affie said, and then slapped her hand to her mouth, appalled at what she'd said.

Odinstoy held something out to her. 'Have this.'

Cautiously, Affie held out her hand. Into it, Odinstoy dropped her ancestor string.

Affie stared at it.

Odinstoy sprang up and ran for the airlock, the platform clanging to her steps.

Affie scrambled up, scuffling in rubbish. Her foot slipped on a sheet of bubble-wrap. She ran, but the door of the airlock closed in her face. A robot voice said, 'Airlock sealed.'

Affie hammered at the door, looked for buttons, instructions, anything, that would help her to open it. She yelled for help, but her voice was lost in the blare of another announcement.

A light appeared on a panel by the door. Something hissed, and she looked round wildly. A breeze touched her face. The air was being pumped from the airlock.

'Odinstoy!' She turned and ran across the platform, not caring how it trembled. Seizing the nearest Bonder, she shook her. 'Can you open the airlock?'

'What?'

'The airlock! The airlock! Odinstoy's in it! Open it!'

Infuriatingly, the girl started shouting at other people. Lots of them ran towards the lock. There was one who had a card to open it – but the door wouldn't accept it.

'It won't open while it's in process,' someone else said.

A young man said, 'Is she wearing a breather?'

'What?' Affie said.

He shouted at her, 'A breather, a breather!' He made gestures around his head and face.

'A breathing mask,' someone else said. 'An oxygen mask.'

'No!' Affie said.

All around her, people relaxed. 'That's all right then.'

'All right?' Affie shouted, in fury. 'All *right*?'

'There are sensors – they detect if the people in the lock are wearing breathers – she's not, so the sequence will abort.'

'Then we can open it and get her out.'

The hissing of air stopped. 'There you are!' the young man said. 'The door will open now.'

The boy with the card pushed it into the door-slot again. There was a grinding noise, a loud *clunk*! and the platform beneath their feet trembled. Everyone stood looking at the door, waiting for it to open. It didn't. Affie noticed that the people around her were beginning to exchange nervous glances. A girl said, 'That sounded like—'

Another grinding noise. The slam of a door; and the platform beneath them trembled again. Then the hissing of air.

Now the fear on the faces around her was plain. 'What?' Affie cried.

A girl beside her ducked down her head and whispered,

'The airlock's emptying – but the air's being pumped to *outside.*'

'So?' Affie demanded.

'It means the airlock opened to outside.'

Another grinding noise. Affie's head snapped round as the airlock door, prompted by the pass-card, opened. She looked into the empty airlock chamber.

She clambered inside, shouting, 'Odinstoy!' The oxygen had been pumped out of here, so Odinstoy must be lying on the floor, unconscious. She wasn't, but Affie still looked for her, anyway, crawling about the floor of the chamber, as if Odinstoy might be invisible and she could find her by touch. 'Where is she? Where?'

People looked in at her from the door. 'Gone,' one of them said.

'She couldn't! The air was pumped out – she'd have collapsed—'

'Not straight away,' the young man said. 'It's not that poisonous out there any more. I mean, you will die without a breather, but not for a few minutes.'

'Breather! You said the door wouldn't open if she wasn't wearing a breather!'

'It's not supposed to,' the young man said. 'It's a safety feature.'

'Malfunction,' somebody said.

A malfunction? Affie, sitting on her heels in the airlock chamber, raised her clenched fists, screwed up her face, and yelled, 'Odin!'

Going Down

John sat hugging his knees, and looking at Affie. He saw how beautiful she was, and how graceful, and how delicately the indigo and violet cloud-shapes moved through her hair. He thought: Why are you alive, you bitch, when Odinstoy's dead – my mother – she called me her son. Why is my mother dead?

Affie was teaching Gift his ancestor string, even though Gift – cold, tired, hungry and bewildered – was in no mood to learn.

'And this one is –?'

'Grandmother,' Gift said, without enthusiasm. He was close to crying.

'No! Great-Grandmother! Great-Grandmother! Say it!'

'Great-Grandmother,' Gift whimpered.

'And this one is?' Affie pointed to the medallion. She was hungry too, and dirty and cold and tired, but Gift had to learn his ancestor string. Odinstoy would have wanted him to know it perfectly. This was something she could do for Odinstoy, even though she'd let her down so badly in – well, in every other way. 'Gift! What is it?'

'Grandmother?'

'Good. And the bead is –?'

John looked away. Why wasn't there someone to tell her to leave Gift alone? She wouldn't listen to him, he knew. And she wouldn't mention the stone arrow, because it would only start Gift asking questions about his mother.

The blaring voice through the loudhailer said that she was dead, that her body had been picked up from outside the dome. Gift had managed to sleep through that. No one wanted to tell him.

I made a promise to her, John thought. The card she'd given him, from her phone, was in his pocket.

He stared across at the child. When Gift was grown, he had to give him the card. He'd promised.

He tried to imagine Gift, grown. He couldn't do it.

And himself? He'd be grown too, a man . . . He couldn't imagine that either: couldn't imagine what he'd look like, or be like. But it would happen. Could he really keep the promise through so many years, so many changes?

It was hopeless, couldn't be done . . . But that was what was expected of a bonder: weakness, snivelling, giving up. He'd prove them wrong, as Odinstoy had. He'd made a promise, and he'd keep it.

But when this was over, he'd be a bonder again. He might be sold to anyone. He might grow up to be a house-slave, or he might end up working in the foundries, or mining the asteroids. How was he going to keep the phone-card hidden?

He'd do it. If you wanted to do something, there was

always a way. He'd hide it, move it about from pocket to pocket . . . He'd do it. He'd promised.

What if Gift was sent back to Earth, to his parents?

Well, John thought, he'd just have to find a way to get the card to him. Earn his freedom, travel to Earth . . . He had to smile at his own thoughts.

Not far from him, Cedar said loudly, 'She's not dead. They're lying to us.'

'She went out through the airlock!' one of the girls yelled. 'How could she be alive?'

'Did you see her go?' Cedar demanded. 'Then you don't know, do you? Anyway, she might have had a breather. You don't know.'

Affie and John looked at each other. Affie wasn't bothering to say any more that she had seen Odinstoy go into the airlock, and that she hadn't had any kind of breathing mask. She'd been told that she hadn't actually seen Odinstoy open the lock's outer doors. She was only guessing that she had.

'Then where is she?' Affie had demanded.

'She could be anywhere.'

Affie had spread her arms, indicating the small, crowded platform and the narrow walkways. 'Where?'

'Odin could have helped her escape,' said a girl, very seriously, and others nodded.

Affie had stopped arguing then, her own head full of such conflicting, whirling thoughts that she felt her skull might crack. There had been a malfunction. Machines often went wrong. But Odin had called Odinstoy to Him, she'd said that He had. And the machinery had gone wrong just when – just as the computer system had crashed when they were being questioned on Earth, before they boarded the space flight. There was a God in the machine.

But, no, a coincidence, a chance malfunction. The second one. A coincidence. It had to be. She didn't want to believe, because if she believed, then she had to serve the God.

She was exhausted. 'Let's give up and go down,' she said.

They were shocked. No, they couldn't; they'd be arrested, she'd be sent back to Earth—

'He said – the man with the loudhailer said – that they wouldn't arrest any of you, that they'd listen to everyone and—'

'They're lying!'

'I'm cold,' Affie said. 'I'm hungry. I'm tired. And what are we going to do? Stay up here until we starve? We can't win. And I want to find out what happened to Odinstoy. I'm giving up and going down.'

But they wouldn't let her. They'd actually pushed her back, and refused to let her walk along the walkways. So she'd retreated to the platform and taught Gift his ancestor string.

'They're going,' John said, at last. 'More of 'em are going.'

Affie looked up. There were fewer people on the platform now and some were uneasily sauntering towards the lifts.

Well, this is it, Affie thought. She tied the ancestor string around her wrist and got up, saying to Gift, 'Come on.' To John, she said, 'Are you ready?'

He looked scared, but nodded.

Holding hands, with Gift in the middle, they started towards the lift. This time, no one tried to stop them. Everybody had had enough.

Affie felt calm, yet her heart beat faster and faster. She thought, They'll be waiting for me, at the bottom, outside the lift. And what then? What were Martian prisons like? Or would she be put on the first ship back to Earth? If Odinstoy really was dead, she'd be alone, because Gift hadn't done anything wrong. He wouldn't be travelling with her.

As they waited for the lift, John said, 'I'll be a bonder again.'

You were never anything else, Affie thought – but then remembered how Odinstoy had called him her son, and realised, with slight surprise, that she wasn't the only person whose life was being turned upside down and inside out. 'I'm sorry,' she said.

The lift came. Its doors opened and they stepped inside. And stood there, looking at each other.

'What? What?' Gift said, and stamped his foot. 'Where Mummy?'

John, looking at Affie, pressed the button. 'Going down,' he said.

ODIN'S VOICE BY SUSAN PRICE

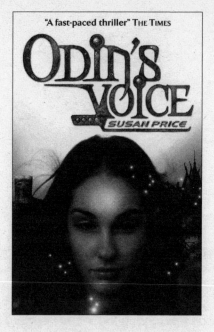

"A fast-paced thriller" THE TIMES

Kylie and Affie, two teens from opposite sides of the track, are thrown together as their roles in society suddenly change.

The great god, Odin, begins to communicate through Kylie, helping her accumulate wealthy patrons and followers as a result, while pampered and precious Affie is made penniless when her father commits suicide. Sold into slavery, she finds herself caring for Kylie's son, 'adopted' by her previous employers. Seeing a way to be reunited with her child, Kylie takes Affie under her wing – and together they plan a dramatic escape...

ISBN 1-416-90144-2 (hardback)
ISBN 1-416-90145-0 (paperback)

SHARP NORTH BY PATRICK CAVE

Mia turned her head sharply... and her eyes met other eyes. A woman, standing amongst the tree shadows across the clearing, watching her.

Then the woman was running towards her and suddenly there was no sound. Two large shapes were moving fast through the trees. Mira heard the slap of snow-heavy branches on fabric and deep, urgent male voices...

Mira lives quietly in a remote community in Scotland – until one day she witnesses a stranger running for her life through the forest. Shot and killed in front of her, the woman's body is quickly removed, the only clue to her death a crumpled piece of paper, and a spot of blood in the snow. Mira discovers the paper contains a list of names, including her own, with another name she recognizes and the word 'watcher' alongside it. Shocked, Mira suddenly begins to view her community with suspicion – and what she discovers throws her whole world into confusion...

ISBN: 0-689-87277-1

IMPERIAL SPY BY MARK ROBSON

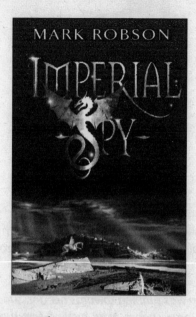

In a world of magic and murder, Femke is entrusted with a vital foreign mission by the Emperor. The task appears straightforward, but the young spy quickly finds herself ensnared in an elaborate trap.

Isolated in a hostile country, hunted by the authorities and with her arch-enemy closing in for his revenge, Femke needs all her wit and skills to survive. Only Reynik, a soldier barely out of training, appears willing to help. But with no knowledge of her true mission, Reynik soon discovers loyalty is a dangerous business.

ISBN: 1-416-90185-X